Lyssa

Lyssa

by

Jerry B. Jenkins

MOODY PRESS

CHICAGO

To Richard Grom

0-8024-4327-3

1 2 3 4 5 6 7 Printing/DB/Year 88 87 86 85 84

Printed in the United States of America

Chapter One

Lyssa Jack had the most beautiful green eyes I had ever seen. So bright, so deep, so brilliant that when she squinted as she listened intently, they seemed to leap out at you. I wouldn't have been surprised to learn that she used dyes or even colored contact lenses.

But she didn't.

"They're all mine," she said, smiling for the first time. "If you ever meet my dad, you'll know where I got them."

Despite her smile, there was a sadness lurking behind those precious eyes. And it seemed to be rooted even deeper than her current problem, the reason she had come to the EH Detective Agency.

My wife, Margo—who has, I'm proud to say, the brown counterparts to Lyssa's green eyes—and our boss, Wally Festschrift, and I agreed to Lyssa's strange request to meet her not in our offices but in a public place.

So, we had met in the parking lot of an Evanston restaurant on a crisp autumn evening. The sun had already set; Margo told me later that she was wondering what Lyssa's lustrous eyes would look like in the light of day. We'd find out soon enough.

Wally, a former Chicago Police Department homicide detective sergeant, had taken over the leadership of the agency from the owner, Earl Haymeyer, when Earl became head of the Illinois Department of Law Enforcement. Wally would have been more comfortable in a greasy spoon than in a spot like Lyssa recommended.

At three hundred plus pounds (he always says, "Two hundred and plenty!"), he finds it difficult to glide into an elegant dining room.

First he nodded to the doorman and reached past him to open the door himself. Then, instead of waiting for Margo and Lyssa to enter, he walked in ahead of them. Margo apologized to Lyssa with a sympathetic look, but it was clear Lyssa's mind was on her business.

As we followed the hostess to our table, Wally again leading the way, the flapping tails of his mammoth trench coat threatened the glasses at the edges of several tables.

"Would you care to check that, sir?" the hostess asked.

"Why? What's wrong with it? Ha! Just kiddin'! Nah, I don't wanna check it. Never could get into payin' to get my own coat off the rack, know what I mean?"

Wally draped his long coat over the back of his chair, leaving a couple of feet of it bunched near the floor. The rest of us checked our coats.

"I didn't mean to be so mysterious by not wanting to come to your office," Lyssa explained. "It's just that if I'm being watched, whoever is watching me will have no idea who you people are. I mean, you're not that well known, are you?"

"No," Wally said evenly, "we're not. Do you think someone is watching you?"

"I don't know. But someone must have been watching Byron before he was abducted. And until I find out who that was and why they did it, I won't know if I'm next or not."

Wally fished a grimy note pad from his pocket. "I'm going to have to ask you to slow down, stop, back up, and start over, Miss, uh —"

"Jack."

"Right. Miss Jack. Name doesn't fit, if you don't mind my sayin'."

"Pardon?"

"Girl pretty as you ought to have a name like Jacques or something."

Lyssa seemed unsure whether to smile or not. So she did.

"So, anyway," Wally continued, "you don't want to be seen goin' into a detective agency, but you think you need our help."

Lyssa nodded. "The police wouldn't do anything, but somebody there recommended you."

"A cop?"

"Uh-huh."

"Remember who?"

She shook her head.

"Who's this Byron?"

"My boyfriend."

"Your boyfriend? How old are you, honey?"

"Twenty-six."

"And Byron?"

"His age?" she asked.

"Uh-huh."

"Thirty."

"And he's your boyfriend, not your fiancé?"

"Well, he is, but I don't have the ring yet, and we won't announce until I have the ring."

"And Byron is missing, is that what you're telling us?"

7

She nodded.

"And you think he was kidnapped, abducted?"

She nodded again.

"What makes you think so?"

"I can't think of anything else, Mr. Fest—"

"Call me Wally."

"Why else would he disappear, Wally?" she asked.

Wally dug into his salad. With his mouth full, he shrugged and said, "There are a lot of reasons people disappear. You want us to find the reasons or the man?"

"The man, of course."

"Give me his name again."

"Byron. Byron Huttmann."

"And who is he?"

"He was an executive with a paper company. Sales Manager. They sell paper to printers."

"Where'd you meet him?" Margo asked.

"At church."

Margo and I flinched. *A Christian?* I wondered.

"Don't jump to any conclusions," she said. "It was my first time in church since high school, and my last."

"You meet your husband-to-be in church but you don't want to go back?" Wally said.

"The man I can take; the church I can leave."

"Until now?" Margo suggested.

Lyssa stared knowingly at her but didn't respond. She turned toward me. "Don't tell me you're all religious?"

I shook my head, because if there's one thing Margo and I don't want to be known as, it's religious. We don't mind being known as Christians, but there's a big difference. Wally mistook the shake of my head and explained.

8

"What he's tryin' to tell you is that they are, but I'm not," he said. "But I'm close, so I guess you gotta say, yeah, we're religious."

"Wally," Margo scolded. "Religion has nothing to do with it, and you know it. That's probably what has Lyssa turned off."

Margo was ready to get into it, but it was obvious that neither Lyssa nor Wally were interested just then. "Margo," he said, "I'm going to ask you to do this on your own time. If this young lady decides to hire us, she's going to be paying a pretty steep fee to hear your pitch."

"All right," Margo said, "I'm sorry. But I can't let you say we're religious without—"

"OK, all right, I know better, you're right," he said with both hands raised. "Miss Jack, these people are religious, but they hate like everything to call it religion, all right? And if you want the rest of the story, you sure know where to get it."

"No, thanks," she said.

Margo's lips tightened, and I could tell she was upset that Wally had shut a door for her.

"Now, back to Byron Huttmann. Why wouldn't the police do anything?"

"Because he's an adult and has a right to do or say anything he wants and go anywhere he wants. He doesn't have to answer to anyone, especially me since we're not officially engaged. They said if I was officially engaged I could sue him for breach of promise or something, but that's the last thing I'm interested in. He didn't back out of anything. He disappeared. And I think he was abducted."

"Why?"

"Why?" she repeated. "Uh, I guess because I can't make any other explanation make sense."

9

"That's not good enough. Has there been any ransom demand, any communication between the abductors and those who would pay to have him returned?"

She shook her head.

"Lyssa, you said he didn't have to answer to anybody, but surely he has to answer to his boss at the paper company. What's the company?"

"Faslund Paper Products on the South Side."

"Is he big enough at the company that he would be worth something to a competitor? Would his company pay to have him back?"

"No. In fact, they're not even concerned."

"An employee disappears and they don't care?" I said.

"They say he didn't disappear. They say he gave them more than the required notice, a whole month. They had a going away party for him and everything."

"And you don't believe it?"

"I don't know what to think."

"How long had you known the man?"

"Almost six months."

"Did you know any of his friends at work?"

"No. I'd never been there."

"Then there is no way you can check out whether they really had a party for him."

"I talked with his boss, the sales and marketing vice president. And I talked to the personnel manager. Both said they had regretfully accepted his resignation and that he had been given the customary send off for an employee who had served the company eight years."

"But now you can't find him," Wally said.

"Right. Even his car is gone."

"His car is gone?" Wally said, incredulous.

"Yes," she said. "Is that significant?"

10

"Well, I should think so," he said. "That tells me he wasn't abducted, unless the kidnapper didn't have wheels."

Margo and I fought not to smile, as did Wally.

"But his apartment was cleaned out too," she said. "Everything gone. It was bare. In fact, two days later it was rented to someone else, even before I could get the police to check it for evidence or anything."

Wally intertwined his meaty fingers over his nearly bare plate. He stared at the beautiful young Lyssa. "I have to tell you, dear," he said. "I think you're naive."

"I'm naive?" she said.

He nodded. "A man whose car and furnishings are gone has not been abducted. A man who gives his employer a month's notice has not been kidnapped. Now, he may be running from something or someone, but no one has taken him against his will. He finished his business with his company and his landlord. His bills are likely paid up. He's just moved on."

Lyssa sat slumped in her chair, shoulders sagging. "He had a good job, a nice place, and he was in love," she said. "He had a future. Why would he leave on his own? I can't buy it."

"I'm not asking you to buy it, Lyssa," Wally said. "In fact, I'd love to dig into it and find out all I can for you. But I would want you to know from the beginning that you might not like what we turn up. It could cost you a lot of money to find out something you don't really want to know."

"I'm not afraid of the truth," she said. "I may be naive like you said, and maybe down deep I have a fear that he might have left on purpose without telling me,

11

but I'd rather know than wonder. You know what I mean?"

"Do I know what you mean?" Wally said. "I make my living because of what you just said."

"I want you to know something else," Lyssa said. "I will accept the fact that he may not have been abducted. But until you prove otherwise, I have to believe that he was pressured to leave. He was threatened, endangered, blackmailed or whatever, but he did not leave on his own."

"Yet he knew he was leaving," Margo said. "At least a month in advance."

It was apparent that Lyssa had been put off by Margo with the talk of being religious, and this mild challenge to her theory was not well received either. Lyssa pointedly ignored her remark.

"He was coerced into leaving," she said flatly. "And I want to know where he is."

"How badly do you want to know?" Wally asked.

"Badly enough to be able to afford your fee."

"For how long?"

"If it's what I've heard it is, at least two weeks."

"That's not much time."

"How well I know," she said, pulling her checkbook from her purse. "I'd like to pay the first week in advance."

"That's not necessary."

"It's what I want to do."

Wally told her the figure for the first week.

"Let me adjust my calculation a bit," she said. "Maybe I can afford only ten days."

"That's tougher."

"I know, but you're the best."

"Who told you that?"

"Chicago cops. They right?"

" 'Course."

"You have ten days to prove it."

"Can we start tomorrow morning at our office? We'll need to know as much about you and Mr. Huttmann as we can."

"I'll be there," she said.

Chapter Two

"You don't have a problem being seen in our office?" Wally asked.

"I guess not," she said. "If you're sure I'm not being watched."

"I couldn't guarantee that. Even so, it won't hurt to throw a little scare into him or her, if you *are* being followed. What's wrong with lettin' 'em know you have help on your side?"

That night in our apartment, Margo was stewing about Wally. "I love the man," she said, "but he does have a way of messing things up, the most important things too."

"I know," I said, deep in thought about Lyssa Jack and her disappearing boyfriend.

Margo paced as I sat on the couch and stared out the picture window into the darkness. "It's not like there aren't enough barriers. I mean, the girl went to church, met her man in church. She apparently got turned off somehow, probably because they pushed ceremony or laws or something instead of emphasizing Christ."

"Uh-huh," I said.

"So now he has to put it to her that I'm going to be trying to convert her to a religion-less faith, something he calls a pitch, and she knows I have to do it on my time, not hers. Terrific."

"Yeah," I said.

"I wonder if this Byron, what's his name — ?"

"Huttmann."

"Yeah, Huttmann. I wonder if he's a Christian or just a churchgoer or if he was there for his first time in years too."

"I wonder."

"Well, Philip, it'll be an uphill battle. Any ideas?"

"Tomorrow will be key," I said, answering the wrong question.

"You mean the impression we make on her?"

"Uh-huh. We have to know all about him."

"Philip!" she said. "I'm talking about sharing Christ with her, not the case."

"I know," I said, not convincing her. "Tomorrow is key to that too. What's your plan, now that Wally got in the way? Let's face it, Mar, it's never easy. But not even Wally Festschrift can get in God's way if He wants to get through to Lyssa Jack."

Margo stopped pacing and flopped down beside me on the couch. "Always wise," she said.

"Hm?"

"You speak wisdom without knowing it."

"Aw, c'mon, Margo. Give me a little more credit than that."

"No, I just mean that I can't get in God's way either, and in fact I might do better to consciously stay out of His way."

"Meaning?"

"Meaning she'll be just waiting for me to jump in with a sermon. And I won't oblige."

"What'll you do?" I asked.

"Love her to death."

"Sounds like a plan."

* * *

15

The next morning the sun picket-fenced its way through the vertical blinds in our outer office and occasionally shone directly into Lyssa's eyes. Margo had been right. They were luminescent in the daylight.

"I'm a nobody," she began, as the three of us sat in a half circle in front of her, and Bonnie, our matronly receptionist, listened in from near the entrance.

"What'sat mean?" Wally asked.

"I'm from nowhere, I've been nowhere, I never did anything, never met anyone important, nothing."

"You graduate from high school?" Wally asked.

"Who didn't?"

"*I* didn't," he said, with more than a hint of pride. "But I don't consider myself a nobody."

"I didn't graduate from college," she said. "Went a little over a year to a community college and dropped out."

"You got brothers and sisters?"

"One each. A brother a lot older and a sister a lot younger. Hardly knew either of them. We get together with my father a couple of times a year and scream at each other about who was responsible for my mother's early death. None of us was. Maybe Dad was. Nobody looks forward to those reunions, but we all always show."

"You look forward to 'em you say?" Wally said.

"No, I said nobody looks forward to them."

"And you're nobody, so you look forward to 'em."

"I get it," she said, not smiling. "Cute. For a big daily fee I get a big daily comedian."

Wally's smile froze. So did Margo's. So this was more than a pretty face with a problem and a dose of naiveté. I knew Margo wanted to jump to Wally's defense, but she was trying her own strategy.

"I think you're special," she told Lyssa.

16

Lyssa looked puzzled and stared, head cocked, at Margo, as if she'd just heard something stupid and couldn't make it compute. Margo plunged ahead. "You are a beautiful girl. You dress well. You apparently have a good job." Lyssa started to protest, but Margo kept going. "You're smart, articulate, witty, sarcastic. Probably well read. You carry yourself with class. You love someone. You care about him deeply enough to make sacrifices to find him. You can't fool me, Lyssa. You may believe you're a nobody, but I never will."

For a moment, Lyssa was speechless. Then she mumbled, "I used to read a lot. Not much anymore. I just work in an insurance office, that's all."

"You're from where?" Wally asked.

"Elkhart, Indiana," she announced wryly, a touch of sarcasm creeping in again. "Recreational vehicle capital of the world. When the economy gets tight and RVs become luxuries, we lead the nation in unemployment. When things turn brighter, the *Tribune* calls us America's boom town. I got out as fast as I could and came to the big city. Chi-town. Fortune, fame, and a man. One out of three isn't bad, if you can hang on to him."

"Tell us about him," I said.

"Traverse City, Michigan," she said. "A storybook case. Salutatorian of his high school class, captain of two varsity sports, studied business at the University of Michigan, graduated with high honors. Recruited by Faslund when he was a senior, started as a sales trainee. Finished his MBA nights at the University of Chicago and kept getting promoted. Never married. Too career oriented. Must have broken a lot of hearts. A real looker."

She produced a picture that could have come from a cologne ad. I said so.

17

"Oh, sure," she said. "He could have modeled. I never felt worthy of him."

"I was just going to say," Margo said, "that you must have made one striking couple."

"All I know is, I believed him when he told me I was the only woman he ever loved. That's why I'm not giving up until I find him."

"What happens when the money runs out?" Wally asked.

"Then I'll work some more and come back looking for a few more days of your time. Or I'll do it on my own. I won't give up."

"He's your whole life," Margo said.

"You got that right," she said. "You heard my story. That's the extent of it."

"But you must have broken a few hearts in your day too," I said.

"Thanks," she said, "but not really. I never let a relationship get far enough so either of us could get hurt. I didn't respect guys who had the poor judgment to ask me out a second time, so I usually turned them down. Only a couple of times I didn't, but I lived to regret it."

"There you go again," Margo said gently. "Running yourself down. I think you're transferring your own poor self-image to the guys who asked you out. Since you had yourself convinced you weren't worthy of them, they had to have bad taste to think otherwise. I'm surprised you survived the cycle in Byron's case."

Lyssa pressed her lips together to keep them from trembling. "Byron was a take-charge guy," she said. "He wouldn't take no for an answer. I fell madly for him the first time I met him, but when he asked me out, I said no. Said it three different times before he insisted and told me when he was going to pick me up. I turned him down probably a dozen times after that, trying to convince him he was too good for me."

"You told him that?" Margo asked, incredulous.

"No, the opposite. That's how I always worked. I insinuated that I had no interest, that he was riff-raff. That had always worked in the past. I never had anybody call me back after an act like that. But Byron did. He wasn't buying the package."

"Because he knew better?"

"Yeah, but not that he thought he was somebody special. He just saw through me. The reason that what you said hit me so hard, Margo, is that it's almost exactly what he said once. He could see to the core of me. I couldn't hide from him. And after a while, I didn't want to."

"How did he handle you?"

"Like a queen. A spoiled queen, perhaps, but a queen. He decided that I was a project worthy of his attention."

"Did you like that?"

"Not at first. I wasn't sure where he was going with it. I didn't want to feel like a challenge, an ugly duckling, a charity case. I fought him at every turn, but I couldn't get enough of him."

"In what way?"

"He was so gentle and kind. He always treated me like royalty. Never came on to me, never was suggestive, even after it was clear we were in love. I don't know how many guys tried to get next to me on first dates. He never did, not even after we had talked marriage."

"Tell me about his family," Wally suggested, clearly not comfortable dwelling on their love relationship.

"I met his brother once. He also has two sisters. He's the oldest. I was to meet his parents next month. His father recently retired, and they're all well-scrubbed middle-Americans from what I can gather. Sort of a *Leave It to Beaver* family as opposed to my *Gilligan's Island* crew."

"What do they say about his disappearance?"

"I don't know if they know."

Wally appeared frustrated. "Excuse me," he said, a little too loudly, "but am I the only one here who thinks it sounds a little strange that you would hire a private detective agency before checking to see if the man didn't head home? I mean, how many Huttmanns can there be in Traverse City, Michigan, forevermore?"

"I didn't say I didn't try to call them," she said. "I just got no answer. I think they're on vacation. It's just the two of them, Mr. and Mrs. Huttman, at home now, you know, and they have means."

Wally rubbed a palm over his mouth. "Where have you looked for this guy?" he asked. "Or where would you suggest we start?"

"I started with his buddies. He didn't have many. A few guys from his church and a couple from the office. The ones from the church said they had no idea he was quitting his job or moving. The guys at work said that when his resignation was announced, they were so shocked and he seemed so reluctant to talk about it, they figured he'd been fired. And a guy of his caliber isn't fired without some big reason."

"But his boss and the personnel manager didn't say he was fired?"

"They said the opposite. They said he had resigned for personal reasons and would let them know when he found other work. No hint of his moving, leaving the area, going to another job, anything."

"I want to know more about his church," Margo said.

20

"I thought you might," Lyssa said, but her smile showed that Margo had already thawed her somewhat. "I went once, like I said. A girl at work had been bugging me to go with her for ages, but I figured if they were all like her, I didn't want to get within a mile of the place. We're talking Polyester City. She was the type who wore her hair in a bun, carried a Bible to work, only wore hose in the dead of winter. You know the type. I was raised in a family full of them. I think she sensed why I was never finding the time to go with her, so she tried a different tack. She said she would introduce me to the sales manager of a giant corporation, and she described him.

"Well, I wasn't ever going to admit that I was coming just to meet this hunk, but it *was* the reason, when I finally got around to accepting. Talk about feeling out of place. And talk about a guy who seemed comfortable though out of his element. It was obvious he was way ahead of these people, you know? Yet they loved him. They didn't resent him or his car or his clothes or his money. I guess because he wasn't one who flaunted it."

"And you fell for him immediately," Margo said.

"Quicker than that. But I couldn't get out of that church fast enough."

Chapter Three

"I hate to be predictable," Margo said, "but I have to ask. What made you so uncomfortable in that church?"

"I was raised in a church like that," Lyssa said. "I know their game. They get you feeling guilty and worldly, and then they move in for the kill. No one can slide by in a church like that. It's all dos and don'ts and fit in and be one of us and don't do anything fun."

We sat in silence for a moment. "Were you there long enough to find out if it was the same as the church you grew up in?" Margo asked finally.

"It doesn't take long to tell," Lyssa said. "They dress the same, spout the same platitudes, offer the same greasy-fingernailed handshakes, the same sickeningly sweet smiles."

"Bet you were surprised to find a guy like Byron Huttmann there," I said.

She grunted. "That's true enough. He stuck out like a sore thumb."

"How can he stand it if it's so bad?" Margo asked.

"Believe me, I asked him that more than once."

"Really? You fought about it?"

"Did we ever!"

"He was what you would call devout, then?"

"Oh, yeah. Sure. Talked about the Lord a lot. Not to

22

people he didn't think were born again, unless he was—what do you call it?—witnessing? Yeah, unless he was witnessing. But with me and with his church friends, the born againers, it was as natural as anything for him to pray before eating, even in public, and talk about God and the Lord and all that."

"What did you think about that?"

"I thought it was fine for him, because apparently he believed it and was serious about it. But it wasn't and isn't for me."

"How did he feel about your attitude toward church?"

"I kept it from him at first, but he was too smart for that. I would hold his hand when he prayed before a meal, but I would never pray when he asked me to. I was always busy on Sundays when he wanted me to join him at church. Finally he told me to keep a Sunday open, but I wouldn't. That's when all the discussions, and eventually the arguments, started."

"Did you ever tell him exactly how you felt?"

"Sure. I wasn't afraid to argue my points, but I avoided it as long as I could because I knew he'd be disappointed. What does all this have to do with the case?"

"Yeah," Wally said, shifting his bulk impatiently. "Let's get into something that's gonna help find this guy."

"This *is* going to help find him, Wally," Margo insisted. "Unless Lyssa left something out of this story, we've got a guy here who has a serious problem in his relationship. He's in love with a girl who doesn't share his view of God, and Christ, and the church. That may not sound like much to you, but it's terribly significant to a lifelong Christian. Am I right, Philip? Didn't you go through the same thing with me?"

23

"Sort of, though I wasn't really in love with you—at least, I didn't know it yet—until after you became a Christian."

"Well, hey," Lyssa said, "I didn't say he and I didn't share the same view of God and Christ. I didn't say I wasn't a Christian. All I said was, I couldn't stand his church, and I wasn't as, um, vocal about God as he was."

"So you *are* a Christian?"

"Yeah!"

"How are you defining that?"

"How are *you* defining it, Margo?" Lyssa demanded.

"Let me ask you this way, Lyssa. How do you compare your Christianity with being born again?"

"Well, I wouldn't say I was a born againer. That's a little intense for me. I believe in God, and I believe Jesus was a real person, and I try to do good. I don't think you can ask more than that."

Wally looked bemused, first staring at Margo, then at me, to see where we'd go with that argument. As if remembering her slightly differently planned approach, Margo backed off. "All I want to establish right now is, you and Byron had widely differing views of what it meant to be a Christian."

Lyssa shrugged. "I wish I could argue with you, but I can't. It's true. Byron didn't think I was a Christian at all. That bothered me to no end. I was mad. I still am. He was wrong, that's all. You can't force everyone into the same mold. I never tried to say he wasn't a Christian or that all those people in his church weren't Christians. They're Christians in their own way, and I'm a Christian in my own way. If they want it their way, that's fine. They just shouldn't expect everybody to get in line for a polyester doubleknit suit."

"Byron didn't wear polyester," Margo said softly.

24

Lyssa scowled and Wally broke in again.

"Awright, where are we?" he said. "I mean, this is all very interesting, but where has it gotten us?" No one spoke, even though both Margo and I believed it had gotten us somewhere, not just in our strategy with Lyssa but in the case as well. Wally said, "I've taken a few notes, and I have some assignments."

"Just a minute, Wally, please," Margo said. "Let me just add something, OK?"

He nodded.

"I don't think we can discount too easily the major problem in the relationship here. Unless Lyssa can say that this discussion, this longstanding argument over their faith, was ever resolved, I think it's significant. I think it could easily relate to his disappearance."

"What?" Wally said. "He leaves her because she doesn't agree with him? A long shot."

"No, it isn't. This is an important matter, especially to a devout believer like Byron seems to have been. He knows he can't marry Lyssa unless they're agreed on this, yet he's in love with her. He has to get away from her because the longer he's near her the harder it will be to pull away when he knows he has to."

"Which is when?" Lyssa asked.

"Before your engagement."

"We *are* engaged."

"Before it's official. Something tells me that a guy like Byron Huttmann has the wherewithal to buy you any diamond he chooses any time he wants. Wouldn't he have good credit?"

"The best. He makes more than fifty thousand dollars a year, lives in a comfortable but not terribly expensive apartment, and pays cash for almost everything, including his car."

"So what's the holdup on your ring?"

25

Lyssa looked down and we could hardly hear her. "You're right," she said.

"Who's right?" Wally said, leaning forward to hear better.

"Margo," she said softly. "I knew he was stalling, hoping I'd come around and see the light. But I didn't. I wouldn't. I fought him on it, and he told me it might mean the end of us. I asked him if he wanted me to embrace his brand of Christianity just to please him. He said no. I said if that was what it took to win his heart, I'd do it, but I couldn't guarantee how long it would stick. He said it wouldn't stick at all. It would be the wrong motive. He said I'd already won his heart. I accused him of just feeling sorry for me. He said he did only in relation to my faith. He said Christ wanted to win *my* heart."

Her monologue had even gotten to Wally, whose eyes were red. "How did you react to that?" he asked, his voice thick.

"I told him he and God were going to have to accept me the way I was. He said he was afraid neither of them would. That hurt."

"Did he clarify what he meant?" Margo asked.

"Oh, yes. I know the whole story. I can come as I am to Jesus, but not expecting to stay that way. But I don't want to change. You see, I like me the way I am."

"But you said you were a nobody," I said.

"But not a bad person."

"I like you just the way you are too," Margo said, putting a hand gently on Lyssa's shoulder. Lyssa looked at her, fighting tears, until Margo added quietly, "But I'm not God."

"You sound like Byron," Lyssa said. "That's all I need, another Byron."

"Yeah, well, listen," Wally said, standing and clapping and moving toward his own office, "pretty soon, on her own time, Margo's gonna tell ya lotsa stuff that'll sound just like it came from Byron, because it's obvious they're cut from the same cloth, isn't it? She'll tell you how you can't get around that verse where Jesus says He's the only way to God. Where's'at, Mar?"

"John fourteen-six, but Wally—"

"Yeah, and the one about the fact that it's all by grace and not by anything we can do. Where's'at one, Mar?"

"Ephesians two, eight and nine, but—"

"But meanwhile, we've got work to do and I'm gonna ask Philip and Margo to join me in my office for some assignments and Miss Jack to leave unless she has anything else to add."

Lyssa pulled on her coat. The rest of us stood waiting to see what she might say. She was clearly distraught. "It's Tuesday," she said. "He's been missing since Friday night. If the only person I ever loved, the only person who ever really loved me, the only reason I have to live, could leave me because I don't fit into his Christian mold—"

"Hey, I didn't say he did," Margo said, as Lyssa headed for the door. "I was just trying to establish that it's a more serious problem in your relationship than you might have thought. And he might be running from his love for you."

"That doesn't make sense!" she said, opening the door.

"It makes a lot of sense!" Margo called after her, moving toward the door herself.

But by now, Lyssa was bounding down the stairs.

"I don't know, Margo," Wally said back in his office. "I know you know a lot more about this stuff than I do, but I can't say I agree that this guy has a motive for running out on his girl friend."

"But I'm not saying he's running out on her. He's running from himself. He's sees trouble ahead. He's in love with someone who's off limits to him. And he's more interested in his relationship with God than with landing this beautiful wife."

"He sounds like a priest."

"In that sense, maybe he is like a priest. He's not interested, even in a lovely girl like Lyssa, if she would in any way damage his relationship to God."

"And it would," I said.

"It sure would," Margo said.

Wally sat shaking his head. "What do we do with this if you're right? If the guy has left on his own, we can't drag him back to her. He has a right to dump his girl friend. This may be a cowardly way to do it, but he's a grown man. I just can't see him giving up his job and his church and his friends and his new hometown because of it. Why didn't he just tell her to get lost, that he'd lost interest in her, that it was over?"

"Maybe he thought this would hurt her less," Margo suggested.

"You're a woman. You tell me," Wally said. "Would this hurt less?"

"No."

"The one thing we still need," I said, "is some evidence that he telegraphed this, that there were some clues, no matter how small, that she would recognize in retrospect. It took her completely by surprise, apparently, but was something said or done during their last few times together that would hit her now as evidence that he was ready to bolt?"

"Yeah," Wally said. "I wonder what the last thing was he said to her. She didn't tell us that, did she?" We shook our heads. "Margo, I want you to find that out, maybe later today if you can reach her. Meanwhile, here's what I want each of you to do."

I was to talk with his employers at Faslund Paper and try to determine if there wasn't something more to his resignation than met the eye. "It just doesn't make sense that his company would let him go, a guy like that," Wally said. "Seems they would have done whatever they had to do to keep hold of a home-grown talent like that."

Margo was to track down his landlord and his friends, either from work or from his church, and also his family. "Somebody has to know something," Wally said. "People don't just disappear off the face of the earth. I mean, who moved him? Did he rent a truck? Where'd he go? He sell everything, or what?"

"What are you going to be doing, Wally?" Margo asked.

"Supervising," he said with a twinkle.

"I wish you would," she said. "Problem is, you're too much of a detective to just be the boss. You'll have your nose in this somewhere and will probably have it figured out while we're chasing wild geese. C'mon, Wally, what'll you be doing?"

He stood and gave her a bear hug. He winked at me over her shoulder and held her so tight she couldn't pull free. "Supervisin'," he repeated. "Now get to work."

Chapter Four

Jo DeMarco, a smart-looking, black-haired, and severe young woman, was personnel manager and quite obviously a climber at Faslund Paper on Chicago's South Side.

"How may I help you?" she asked without a smile when her secretary told her that I had insisted on talking with her directly. "I believe Vivian made it clear to you that we do not discuss employees with outsiders."

I showed her my card, which elicited only a raised eyebrow. She handed it back to me. "You may keep it," I said.

"No, thank you, Mr. Spence. I believe I'll be able to remember your name, your firm, and your position for the duration of this conversation."

Oh, that was smooth. I liked that. I grinned from ear to ear to show my appreciation, but Ms. DeMarco stared me down. "Well, ah, let me ask you some questions and see if you are allowed to answer any of them at all, may I?"

"You may ask, and it's not a matter of being allowed to answer. I'm dealing with the law here, Mr. Spence, and if you are who you say you are, you are well aware of the laws governing what can or cannot be shared by employers."

"That would be 'what *may* or *may* not be shared,'
wouldn't it, Ms. DeMarco?"

"Whatever."

"In other words, you may not, but you *could*,
couldn't you?"

"Of course I could. But I won't. Is there anything
else?"

"Perhaps if I told you why I want information about
Mr. Huttmann, you would feel freer to discuss him."

Suddenly Jo DeMarco looked plainly shaken. "I'm
sorry, I didn't realize that you were requesting information about Byron Huttmann. Certainly, I can tell you
whatever you need to know, within reason. I have been
given full authority to do that and to give him the
highest recommendation from the firm. And I mean
from the top."

"Excuse me?" I said, merely stalling to make this all
make sense. I thought I would be dealing with Miss
Fort Knox, and all of a sudden she was falling all over
herself to cooperate.

"You needn't feel obligated to tell me what firm you
represent. We know you need a recommendation, and
we guessed that it would be sought in this manner,
through a private agency I mean. So, ask anything you
wish."

"In all honesty, Ms. DeMarco, I'd love to take
advantage of whatever incorrect assessment you've
made of me, but I have to tell you that I represent the
name on the card, that's all. There are personal and
private reasons for asking about Mr. Huttmann, and I
would be remiss if I implied anything else."

"Duly noted," she said, as if I had just recited
something for the record. "What would you like to
know about Mr. Huttmann?"

"Whatever you have."

31

She pulled a four-by-six card from a file next to her desk and read from it. "Byron Norrin Huttmann, born August 5, 1953, Traverse City, Michigan. Graduate of Traverse City High School, June 1971. Salutatorian. GPA three-point-nine-six. Graduate of the University of Michigan, May 1975, bachelor of science degree, majored in business. Hired June 1975 as sales management trainee. Promoted August 1976 to sales representative. Promoted November 1977 to regional sales manager. Promoted January 1979 to district sales manager. Promoted April 1980 to assistant national sales manager. Promoted January 1981 to national sales manager. Gave written and oral notice of resignation Friday, September 30, 1983, to become effective Friday, October 28, 1983. Due to exemplary record of service to the company, Mr. Huttmann received six months' severance pay."

"Wow," I said. "He really slowed down after he became national sales manager, didn't he?"

Finally I had coaxed a smile from Ms. DeMarco. "Anything else?" she asked.

"I'm curious to know what reasons he gave for his resignation."

"Personal. Not specific."

"What kind of measures did his superiors go to to persuade him to stay?"

"You would have to discuss that with the sales and marketing vice president. I can tell you, however, that I was in the middle of it and it involved many after-hours meetings, messages being run back and forth between his apartment and the office on the weekends, and similar efforts. I believe the president himself was involved in much of the negotiation."

"But no one knows why he wanted to leave?"

"Not really. We all assumed he would be trying to

determine his worth on the open market and encouraged him not to leave before he found something else."

"How was the severance arrived at?"

"Mostly it was due to the fact that he rarely took more than six or seven days off a year. We were afraid you might wonder about the severance, with the possibility it would make the parting appear to be a termination."

"Well, it *is* unusual, you must admit."

"Unusual isn't the word for it, Mr. Spence. It's unique to this company. I've never seen it given anywhere under these circumstances."

"How do you account for it?"

"He was a superstar; what more can I say? No one fought it. No one. Not even payroll, and certainly not personnel. He was an idol of mine. He was an example to all the young employees of what was possible if you did your homework, kept your nose clean, did your job, worked hard."

"No one resented him?"

"I wouldn't say no one. It's always hard when a young man moves up quickly, but certainly no one who worked over him or for him."

"Does anyone have any idea where he is or where he's going?"

"I was just about to ask you that, Mr. Spence. I'm a good confidence keeper, and I figured that when you had gotten all you wanted from me, you might tell me what company you represent and what position Byron is being offered."

"You don't seem to understand, Ms. DeMarco. I don't represent any company except the agency I work for. We are representing an individual client who feels that Mr. Huttmann disappeared. We're trying to locate him. That's all."

33

She smiled, as if not believing me. "I hope you're joking," she said. "I am not allowed to give out the information I gave you, especially the supplementary comments."

"I appreciated it and will not break your confidence. Frankly, if I had been representing a company looking into hiring Mr. Huttmann, I certainly would want to pursue him. But nothing you gave me is of any use in finding him, as far as I can tell."

Jo DeMarco's eyes narrowed and the smile vanished. "Are you serious?" she said.

"I never tried to imply otherwise," I said.

She squinted at me, as if wondering what to think. "I don't believe you," she said. "But just in case you're telling the truth — in fact, even if you're not — I'll tell you where I think Byron is. I think he's bought himself an unbelievable spread somewhere way up on the North Shore and is negotiating with some obscenely huge corporations. He may even wind up executive vice president or president, who knows? He could do it. Now, after that careful assessment, won't you tell me which one it is, or do you represent more than one?"

By now I was enjoying the game, even though I hadn't intended to play. "If I was representing one of the biggies, would I tell you?" I asked.

"Fair enough," she said. "I guess not. I should have gotten a promise to trade information before I offered mine."

"But you were under direct order of the president."

"Forget I said that. If you are who I think you are, it's all right, but if you're not, you can just forget everything I told you here today."

"I'll try not to."

"Then you *are* who I think you are."

34

"No, I'm afraid I'm not, if you think I'm a headhunter, or working for a headhunter. But I'm paid to remember everything you told me, and you can believe I will."

She was still looking a bit cockeyed at me when I asked if I could talk to Byron Huttmann's most recent superior. "Certainly," she said. "That would be T.J. Hindley-Worth, and you'll find him on the twenty-seventh floor. I'll let him know you're coming."

I wished she wouldn't, but I don't suppose I would have been able to secure an appointment with him otherwise. I was able to slip onto an express elevator with a maintenance man who informed me that the car was only for maintenance. I nodded and moved slowly to get off when the doors shut, and we whizzed straight to the twenty-seventh floor.

I whirled around, quickly scanning the names on the doors and burst into the outer office of Mr. Hindley-Worth. At least I assumed he was a he. I asked if he was in. "He's on the phone right now, Mr. —"

"Spence."

"If you'll have a seat, Mr. Spence —"

"Could I use your phone for just a second, please? Thank you."

Before she could protest, I reached past her, picked up the receiver, and punched several of the push buttons. Before taking my hand away I switched to Mr. Hindley-Worth's line and heard him say, "Now, Jo, you know the man is with one of the big firms, no matter what he says. You did just fine, and I'll do the same. Thanks for the tip."

I hung up when he did, thanked her, and was taking a seat when she said, "I'll tell him you're here, but without an appointment, I can't promise —"

From the intercom came her boss's voice. "Liz, when a, uh, Philip Spence arrives, send him in, will you?"

"He's on his way, sir."

T.J. Hindley-Worth was pulling on his suit coat and straightening his tie as I entered. It made me wish I was representing a bigger firm, checking out the talent at Faslund. Here he was, at least twenty years my senior, wearing a five-hundred-dollar suit and occupying a lavish office, yet he seemed intent on making a good impression.

"Mr. Hindley-Worth, I'm Philip Spence with the EH Detective Agency in Glencoe," I said, shaking his hand.

He was a ruddy, freckle-faced, stocky man with too-long dark blond hair expensively done. "Glencoe!" he said. "Well, sit down, sit down." He made sure to come around to the front of his desk and join me at a small conference table. He knew better than to pull one-upmanship on a talent evaluater. "And please, call me T.J. No formality in this office."

I glanced around and had to wonder. The four-feet in diameter globe and four posh wing-backed chairs certainly lent an air of formality and authority to the room. "Thank you, T.J.," I said. "I know you're a very busy man, so I'll come right to the point. I need to know whatever I can about Byron Huttmann, your former—"

"National sales manager, of course. May I inquire as to the reason for your interest?"

"Purely a personal matter. Our client simply wants to locate him, that's all."

"Locate him? Well, I understand he recently moved out of his apartment, but I don't know where he went. I'm sure personnel could tell you his new address because they will have reason to be in touch with him by mail over the next few weeks."

"Ms. DeMarco was very helpful, and I'll ask her for that as well, thank you."

"That clear it up, then?" he asked with a twinkle, apparently thinking that with his action orientation he had clearly exposed the fact that I wanted more than just to locate his former employee.

"Ah, no," I said. "If you have a couple of more minutes."

"Sure do," he said.

"Do you know any reason why Mr. Huttmann left the company so suddenly?"

"I can assure you it was of his own accord. We have nothing but the highest regard for him and would give him the highest recommendation for whatever he chose to pursue."

"Thank you, but are you simply assuming that he's testing the market for his skills?"

"Well, yes, I think so. I don't think it was the wisest thing to do before having something nailed down, but apparently it hasn't hurt him, know what I mean?"

"No, I don't."

"Well, I mean, let's not play games with each other, Mr. Spence. We both know why you're here. And when a firm procures the services of a top notch private investigating agency to check on the history of a candidate, why, it's pretty apparent that he's up for quite a good job with a very large corporation. If you were to feel you could divulge just which one, you could certainly count on my confidence — "

"No, I'm afraid I'm not at all prepared to share that information," I said. He fought a grin, assuming more from my statement than I meant to imply. But again, it seemed I should roll with it. "How about yourself, T.J.? You ever get restless, or is it safe to assume you're pretty well entrenched here?"

"Me? Oh, ha! Well, yeah, they take care of me pretty good, if you know what I mean. Can't complain. I wouldn't say I'm married to the place, though I'm a very loyal guy. I think I've reached my level here, not that I'm not capable of something more. It's just that given the structure and the personnel here, I'm probably as high as I'm going to get. There are times when I get the itch to test the waters a bit myself. Why do you ask?"

"Just curious. What would have happened to you if Mr. Huttmann had stayed on board?"

"Oh, he probably would have passed me up. I think we'd all have been working for him someday. Maybe we still will, right? You know? Maybe we still will!"

T.J. Hindley-Worth thought that was quite amusing, but I must have missed something.

"T.J.," I said, "if you hear from Mr. Huttmann, would you call me?"

"Sure enough! And listen, just between you, me, and the fence post, you run across any choice spots in the course of your business that you think might be my cup of tea, you give me a call on the Q.T. too, huh?"

"I'll sure do that," I said, wondering what he would think if he knew how little contact I have with people in his world. "I sure will."

On my way out of the building I stopped in to see Ms. DeMarco one more time. She still barely hid that smug smile that told me she knew who I really was even if I wasn't admitting it. I told her the vice president said she would give me Mr. Huttmann's mailing address.

While her secretary was digging for it, I said, "Jo,

38

you said Byron was an idol of yours. Was he an interest as well?"

"What do you mean by that? Was I interested in him personally? No. I mean, well, no, not really. Any woman with two eyes would be naturally intrigued by the man, but he was too much of a holy roller for me. There were few girls around here would have met his list of qualifications."

"He had a list?"

"Not really a list, but ones who went out with him at all wound up going to church with him. He never developed any real relationships with women, here or outside as far as anyone here could tell."

A note in his file, written in his own hand, instructed personnel and payroll to contact him at his apartment address. "The P.O. will forward," it explained.

Chapter Five

On my way home I stopped at the post office in Burbank, the adjoining suburb where Byron Hutt-mann's apartment had been. "I need a forwarding address," I said.

"Fill out the form," a bored, sloppily uniformed old woman said without looking at me. It called for his full name and previous address. I had to look it up in the phone book.

When I returned to the counter I was sixth in line. I switched lines and the position closed. I switched again and drew an angry stare from someone with the same idea. Finally I wound up waited on by the same old woman.

She snatched the card from the counter and held it far from her eyes. "Can't give it to ya," she said, sliding it back to me.

"What do you mean you can't give it to me? I filled out the card."

"I handled that address change myself Saturday," she said. "Nice looking young man. He's forwarding his mail to a box number, but the request is not to give it out. You're the second one asking for this boy today. Popular guy."

"A box number here?"

"I can't tell you that either, son. Sorry. Next?"

"I've never heard of such a thing," I told Margo at home.

"I hadn't either," she said, collapsing in the easy chair in the living room. "Until I found out the same thing from the same woman at the same post office this morning. I suppose it makes sense though. A person ought to have the right to keep his address private if he wants."

"But how long will it last?" I asked. "Surely his address will become known in a few weeks."

"Even a few weeks' privacy from the kind of mail we get would be a blessing, wouldn't it?"

I couldn't argue with that. We agreed not to burden Wally with the news of our overlapping efforts, and she shared my amusement at the people from Faslund and their preening before a detective they thought had been hired either by a huge corporation or by an international headhunting company.

"I spent most of my day with the landlord and then at a Haul-It-Yourself place," she said. "I struck out at the post office and trying to reach anyone in Traverse City, Michigan. Who knows how long they'll be on vacation? Wally said you could help me with church and work friends tomorrow."

"Did you locate any today?"

"One of each from names Lyssa remembered, though she had met only the guy from church. I have appointments for tomorrow."

"You talked to Lyssa since this morning?"

"Yeah."

"You ask her the last thing he said to her?"

"Uh-huh. Are you ready for this? He held her tight

41

and kissed her and told her he would always love her. Looked deep into her eyes, the whole bit."

"Wow," I said quietly.

"Wow is right," she said. "I think I'd look for help finding him too."

"So the landlord said he moved himself, huh?"

"Yeah, and he means by himself. He moved all his own stuff with some sophisticated dollies and carts. A couch, a bed, lots of big stuff."

"Appliances?"

"Don't think so. They come with the apartment. The landlord offered to help or to get some kids to help, but Huttmann politely refused. He asked Huttmann where he was going and he said, 'Oh, not that far.'"

"That helps."

"Yeah, that really pinpoints it, doesn't it?" she said.

"Yeah. The landlord recognized the truck?"

"Right. I tried a couple of local rental places without any luck, then one of the dealers told me to call a toll free number that would hook me up with a national computer. It worked like a charm. They directed me to the next place I would have tried anyway."

I laughed. "And you found something?"

"Yes, something very interesting. Byron picked up a truck on Saturday morning. Showed up in a metallic blue Datsun two-eighty Z, chauffeured apparently by a car salesman. He told the dealer, 'With any luck it'll be sold by the time I get back.' He brought the truck back late that evening with nearly three hundred miles on it, then hailed a cab, but the rental dealer couldn't remember the cab company."

"Easy enough to check. There can't be too many companies servicing that area. He paid his bill all right?"

"Cash. The dealer said he told him that he had drop off points in lots of cities and that if he had known he was going that far, he would have located another dealer where he could have taken the truck."

"How did Byron respond?"

"Didn't say much. Said he didn't mind or something like that."

"We've got to find out where he went in that cab, Margo."

"I'm guessing he went to the car dealership to see if his car sold."

"Maybe. But then we'd have a lead on where he went after that, because he would have needed another ride."

"What I get out of the whole thing so far, Philip, is the fact that this man left on his own. He may have done it quickly and left few traces, but he certainly didn't seem to have a gun to his head."

"We don't know that. He could have been running from someone."

"The only person Byron Huttmann was running from was Lyssa Jack."

"You really believe that, Margo?"

"I do. Don't you?"

"I guess I agree with Wally," I said. "I don't know. It doesn't seem to be enough to make a man throw away his life."

"Oh, I think it does! If he marries her in her current spiritual condition, *then* he throws away his life. If he's in love with her and can't get her to come to Christ, he has to run. It's sad, but I can see it."

"Maybe," I said, "but does he seem like the type to give up so easily? It seems he would jump into this challenge with both feet."

"We don't know how much might have gone on between them. Maybe he gave it all he had, realized he was hopelessly in love, and saw that he had to get out."

"What a price to pay," I said.

"But he'll land on his feet. I don't understand, necessarily, his moving himself, selling his car, bringing the truck back to the original renter and all that, but apparently he's trying to start over somewhere."

We had a pizza delivered and continued discussing the case in our robes.

"His friends said something in common," Margo said. "Each said he didn't know the other well. But each knew that Byron was close to two other people."

"Two? Meaning the other friend and Lyssa?"

"No. That's the interesting part. Neither of them was aware of Lyssa. They knew he dated and that he was often busy on evenings and weekends, but neither knew Lyssa's name."

"You're kidding," I said.

"That's what I said to each. They wanted to know all about her. I told them nothing, of course, but promised I would give them a little more when we talked tomorrow."

"We'll have to be careful about that."

"I know."

"So each knew Byron was close to the other and to one other person. Who?"

"Collin J. Walsh, apparently a mucky-muck at Fas-lund."

"A mucky-muck indeed. Walsh is the president."

"Really, Philip? Are you sure? Maybe that's why the one from his office said something about Byron's being so careful of that relationship, avoiding jealousy and things like that."

44

"Do these guys think Byron is closer to Walsh than to either of them?"

"Oh, yes. They believe Walsh is a father figure, a confidant that they have never been able to match. They seem to be the types who are open and vulnerable and personal with him, but he doesn't really reciprocate."

"That trait doesn't really offend me," Jeff Hertzler told us the next morning at the garage where he worked. "I've known Byron since he joined our church; must have been seven, eight years ago. He's a great softball player. I hope he stays around just for that."

Hertzler was a long, tall, knuckly man in his late thirties who smiled sheepishly and then let his shoulders bounce when he laughed. "I guess I shouldn't have really said that. I would miss him if he was gone, but something tells me he's not really gone. Just left for a while maybe."

"But he never shared much personally with you?" I said. "You weren't aware of his love life?"

"Oh, he didn't have a love life," Jeff said, growing suddenly serious. "I know he would date quite often, but only Christian girls of upstanding character, and usually ones I knew from church. I never saw him with this one you mentioned on the phone yesterday, ma'am. You say you got my name from her?"

"Yes, she's heard of you, Jeffrey," Margo said. "Apparently Byron is quite fond of you and your family."

"He gets a kick out of the boys, that's true, and Alice, her too. Yeah, I'd say we get along good. Not close, you know, but close like Christians can be, you know."

45

"Yes, we know," Margo said. "We're both Christians too."

"No kiddin'? Born again?"

"Yes, sir."

"That's somethin'! And private detectives!" We nodded and smiled. "Then you *do* know what I'm talking about."

We nodded again. "But I am troubled that he didn't tell you more about himself," I said.

Hertzler ground the grease deeper into his hands with an oily rag and leaned back against an engine block. "You know, I don't think that should be so troubling. You see, the man had nothing to hide and nothing to tell, as far as we could see. You can talk to Alice, and she'll tell you the same thing. There was never anything mysterious or secret about the man. He was a good guy, a doer, you know? Helped out a lot on work days at the church, helped with the kids' clubs, was pretty active, played ball.

"Now if he's up and left, that would shock us to death, I think, but other than that, I don't think he kept anything from us, or had anything to keep from us. I know he had himself a pretty good job there, and only because I counted the offerings for a year or so, I know he either makes a pile of money or he gives a whole lot more'n ten percent. Now that's none of my business, nor yours if you don't mind my saying so. Why don't we both just forget I said anything about that. All I'm saying is that he wasn't extra quiet or private or anything. We knew all about his family back in Michigan, and we knew when he was traveling on his job, but he didn't tell us many details about that."

"In what way would you say you were close?" Margo asked.

"Well, he would probably spend more Sunday dinner

46

times with us than anyone else. 'Course we probably asked him more often too. I know he's quite a bit higher up in the world than we are, but that never bothered me if it didn't bother him, and it sure didn't seem to bother him. We played ball in the yard and watched the Bears on TV with the boys. All that stuff. Only time he really ever told me anything about his work was when he told me he had just two good friends there and that neither of 'em was Christians.''

"Who were they?"

"Well, one was somebody who worked in the home office, I guess, who was under Hutt somehow. I usually called him Hutt. He was this guy's boss, but he and him hit it off pretty well and he was tryin' to witness to him and stuff and yet and still he had to watch that he didn't show favoritism to the guy, you know what I mean?"

We nodded.

"The other close friend he had there — and he had to really be careful about this one — was the president of the company. I don't remember his name right off. Alice would if you want to call her. But I know he's spent time at that president's home, which is something most guys in a company like that don't do, I imagine, unless they're there for a party with everyone else or something. He was pretty fond of the old guy, I guess.''

"What gave you that impression?"

"Well, it seemed he spent a lot of time with him. More than you would think, I guess. I don't know. And the old man encouraged him a lot along the way, gave him hints and ideas on how to be a better employee or something. He sure got a lot of promotions there for a while. We had to read about 'em in the paper. He'd never say a word.''

"Never talked about himself much?"

"Not unless the Lord was doing something special in

his life, and then it was always something he'd learned, not something he'd accomplished."

"He sounds just a little too good to be true."

"You know, that's just what Alice says, but she means it in a good way. I mean, she's got women's intuition comin' out her ears, and when she first said that, I says to her, 'You're not sayin' he's a phony, just like that insurance man you had figured last spring,' and she goes, 'Nah. I mean it. This guy really is too good to be true. But I think it's God's doin'.' And so do I, Mr. and Mrs. Spence. I really do."

Chapter Six

Nolan Schwab, Faslund Paper's midwest district sales manager headquartered in the Chicago office, had a different, but surprisingly complementary view of Byron Huttmann.

"I believe the man was raised right," he said in a Tennessee drawl. "Quiet. Kept to himself. Kind of a private individual. A little too religiously zealous for my taste, but you respect a man who is serious about what he believes.

"He was a motivator in his own quiet way. Always did everything thorough. He was ready, prepared, ran the best sales conferences I've ever seen. Everything in place, nothing hanging out to be filled in later. If he said we'd have catalogs and order blanks and paper samples and pitch books at sales conference, we had 'em."

"How did you get close to him?" I asked.

"Well, see, I never really did. I never felt like I really got next to the guy, and I wanted to be careful I didn't look like I was apple polishing. There were times I was tempted to take Byron up on his invitations to church —I was raised Southern Baptist but haven't been back to church in years—but my real motive would have been to find out what made him tick, because he never really seemed to let on. I didn't know why he was so private. Now you tell me you got my name from his fiancée or almost-fiancée—that just about scrambles my brain. I knew he was dating, but I thought he was playing the field. Apparently not, huh?"

"You're seen as someone close to him," Margo persisted. "Did you not consider yourself that?"

"Like I say, I knew we weren't close, but even the bosses need someone in the office to talk to. I was his someone. We went to lunch together. We talked a lot. He knew everything about me and my two marriages and my three kids and my financial situation. Everything. It seemed natural to tell him and have him listen and try to weasel some advice out of him. Nothing was ever volunteered, especially advice. But when it came, it was always right on the money."

"Did he ever talk about Jeff and Alice Hertzler?"

"Not *about* them really, no. I heard their name now and again because he spent a lot of Sunday afternoons with them and their kids. But I never met the couple, and Byron never actually said anything *about* them. Or anybody except his family."

"Not even Mr. Walsh?" I asked.

Nolan Schwab fell silent and studied us. His mouth curled into a slight, closed grin. "Uh," he said in a whisper, "not too many people know the details of Byron's relationship with Collin Walsh."

"You make it sound illicit," Margo said.

"Oh, no, it's anything but that," he said quickly. "It's just that it was the best and the worst thing he had going for him at Faslund. It made the rest of the management team a little wary of him, a little defensive, I guess. And people did talk behind his back about it."

50

"Such as?"

"Oh, you know, accusing him of playing up to the boss. Somehow everyone knew they were fond of each other and socialized, but neither of them ever mentioned it, at least as far as I knew."

"Did you ever ask him about it?"

"Oh, sure. I asked him all about it, and I told him how everyone assessed it. He let his guard down only one time. He just said that usually he didn't initiate the contacts. The old man would invite Byron to join him and his wife and a daughter who still lives at home on an outing of some sort."

"A grown daughter? Was the old man matchmaking?"

"No, no. She's probably forty-five. She supervises the domestic staff at the Walsh estate."

"The staff?"

"I believe there are six full-time people living at the complex."

"The complex?"

"You're surprised? This is a very wealthy family. And I mean old money. They live not far from Lake Michigan on several acres in Kenilworth. I believe there are four buildings besides the main home. There's a gardener, a butler, a maid, a chauffeur (who's half paid by Faslund Paper, I think), a handyman, and a cook."

Margo and I shook our heads. "How do you know so much about the staff?"

"Oh, ha! That does sound weird, doesn't it? Everybody at Faslund knows everything about the Walshes. The old man never says much about himself, so it's a hobby among the employees. Anybody who's ever been out there—I've been there twice myself—comes

51

back with as much as they can find out and trades tidbits. It's fun."

"Tell us more about the immediate family," Margo said.

"He had three children. The daughter at home—I don't remember her name—is the oldest. She was a college art professor and an antiquities expert, so she's more than just an appointments secretary and coordinator. She purchases art for the home, that kind of thing.

"He has another daughter who's some kind of physicist and married well, a doctor I think. Lives in the East. And he had a son who died in a car accident on the night of his high school graduation, ten or twelve years ago. That's when the sister came home to be with her parents for a while. She never left."

Margo and I looked at each other. "The son he lost would have been about Byron's age," I said.

"A lot of people in the company have said that," Schwab said. "That's why maybe they're not quite as hard as they could be on a guy who's that close to the president without even being a vice president. 'Course if the old man made him a vice president before anyone thought he was ready, I suppose there could be morale problems. Thing is, none of the VPs are that close to the chief either."

"Has it appeared that Byron was rising too fast for his or the company's good?"

"Oh, there's always been a lot of talk like that, but the people who've promoted him, when and if they talk about it in private, insist that they had no interference from the top. The only one who carried a grudge about it, I guess, was one of the last guys who promoted him."

"He promoted Byron, yet he holds a grudge?"

"Yeah, well, see, he promoted Byron to assistant sales manager in, ah, nineteen eighty, I guess it was. It was a new position, raised a lot of eyebrows, you know. Well, not a year later, in fact it might have been later that same year. Uh, let's see, it may have been announced late in nineteen eighty but became effective in nineteen eighty-one, the vice president of sales and marketing promoted Byron past his boss. Had them switch titles and responsibilities."

"So, Byron became sales manager and this other guy was demoted to assistant?"

"Right, but not for long. He left to become marketing director of one of our biggest competitors and really did us some damage for a while."

"How?"

"Underpricing us, making us look bad. Making us look expensive. Making Byron look like he didn't know what he was doing."

"But that didn't last?"

"Nah. Byron came up with some creative product and service ideas that allowed us to produce better things at lower prices, and Chomick had to back off and regroup to keep from going under."

"Chomick is the other company?"

"No, Levinthal Paper is the company. Dean Chomick is the guy who left us to work there."

"Can you give us a gut level reaction, Nolan? Where do you think Byron Huttmann is?"

"Gut level?"

"Uh-huh."

"Where I think he is?"

"Right."

"You mean living, or working?"

"Either one."

"I don't have the foggiest, I really don't. I wish I did. If you find him, you'll let me know, huh?"

"I think we're going to start with Mr. Chomick," I said. Nolan Schwab shrugged and nodded.

"I talked with Chomick this morning," Wally said that afternoon at the office as we finished our accounts of the interviews.

Margo threw up her hands. "How did you get onto Chomick before we did?" she asked, admiration overshadowing her frustration.

"From that Huttmann work history Philip rattled off to me, the one he got from the personnel manager."

"Chomick's name wasn't on that list," I said.

"No, but it was pretty clear that someone had been left in the dust by this Huttmann roadrunner. I called the personnel manager and asked her what happened to the sales manager when Huttmann took his job. I says, 'Did he go up, down, or out?' An' she says, 'Down and out.' He wasn't hard to find."

"What did he say?"

"He says he and Huttmann buried the hatchet more'n a year ago. It was Huttmann's idea. Chomick says it was all right with him, but he didn't appreciate the big religious presentation that came with it. He says if he didn't know better, he'd have thought Huttmann was trying to make out like the whole thing was Chomick's fault because he wasn't a churchgoer."

"Did he have any idea where Huttmann would be?"

"No, but he said he'd hire him in a minute if he was available. He said Huttmann was young, disorganized, and a slow decision maker, but if Chomick could put him under his wing, he'd blossom. 'And besides,' he says, 'that would keep any of my competitors from getting him.'"

"He sounds like a real honey," Margo said.

Wally guffawed.

"You think he has anything to do with where Huttmann is now?" I asked.

Wally shook his head. "Nah," he said. "I don't think he really cares where Huttmann is, either."

"So where does all this leave us?" I said.

"It's fairly obvious," Wally said, which hurt.

"Walsh?" Margo said.

"You guessed it," he said. "If he doesn't know anything, we're left with Byron's immediate family. And that means some travel."

"You think he could be in Traverse City?" I asked.

"No, that would be outside this range."

Margo and I looked at each other as Wally produced a huge map of the Chicagoland area, on which he had circled a one hundred and fifty mile radius with the truck rental place in the center.

"If he put a little over three hundred miles on the truck, he couldn't have gone any further than this," Wally said. "And in fact, he probably went a little less. How do we know that?"

We both love it when Wally plays Sherlock Holmes deductive reasoning games, but this one stumped us both. We shrugged.

"I'm disappointed," he said. "Think. He got the truck, then went back to his apartment and loaded it. *Then* he went wherever he was going and came back to the rental place. So, the actual distance from the rental place to wherever he moved could have been considerably less than the three hundred miles."

"As much as twenty-four miles less," Margo said.

"Because his old apartment is twelve miles from where he rented the truck."

"Very good," Wally said. "Philip, why don't you and I talk to the cab company while Margo lines up an appointment for you two with Mr. Walsh?"

"What'sa matter," came the voice of the dispatcher at South Suburban Taxi, "you leave somethin' in a cab?"

"No, sir," I said, "just checking on a fare one of your guys had on Saturday."

"That should be easy," he said. "Only two guys was workin' Saturday. Tell me where and when, and I'll see if I can raise 'em on the box."

I told him and listened as he queried two cabbies over the radio. Neither had worked the area in question during the last week, let alone Saturday.

"Sorry, pal. You sure it was us?"

"Thought so. You only had two cabs on the street Saturday, huh?"

"I didn't say that, buddy. You said one o' my guys. Toni was on drivin' Saturday too, only this Toni ain't no guy."

"Would you mind checking with her?"

"It'll be a while. She just called in that she's eatin'."

"Maybe you could have her call us if she remembers the guy."

"No promises."

"I understand."

"Not real smart," Wally said in his non-threatening way when I was off the phone. "If she doesn't call, that doesn't mean she didn't have Huttmann in her cab."

"How do you figure?"

"All it means is she doesn't have any motivation to call. What does she care? She doesn't even know why you want to know."

56

"Should I have told her?"

"Not necessarily. I'm just saying that if you don't hear from her, don't assume anything. Try to get to her yourself. She may be suspicious of your interest. She might even try to protect him, especially if he tipped her well."

"Sorry."

"There's nothing to be sorry for," Wally said. "Just be sure you talk to her by the end of the day."

I did better than that. She called back less than an hour later.

"I remember the guy," she said. "Good lookin', late twenties. Felt sorry for him. He was hot and tired like he'd been workin' all day. Musta been. I picked him up at the truck rental and took him to a car dealership. Foreign. The one on Cicero. Crazy thing is, he tells me to wait. Comes back to the cab lookin' happy and tells me he just sold his car. Fancy one. I don't remember. Now, he must've got a check, because he asks me to run him over to the tollway, you know, two-ninety-four north."

"What's that got to do with his getting a check?"

"Well, I mean, he musta been out of cash because when I let him off near the expressway, he started hitchhiking. I told him he couldn't hitchhike on the tollway, so he stood on the feeder ramp. I offered to take him anywhere he wanted, but he said no."

"Did he seem upset?"

"Upset? Naw. I'd say the opposite. He seemed happy. More than happy. Like he had just gotten out of jail or something. When I pulled away I could see him in my rearview mirror, lookin' for a ride north on two nine four."

Chapter Seven

Margo had made an appointment for us to see Collin J. Walsh the next morning, but she asked Wally if he would mind if we asked Lyssa Jack to visit us that night. "There are a few things I'd like to ask her before we get too deep into this thing to understand what we're turning up."

Wally agreed, and when Lyssa arrived, Margo jumped right in. "I can't speak for Wally or my husband," she said, "but I don't suspect foul play at this point. A car salesman delivered him to a truck rental place the day he moved out of his apartment, and a cab took him from there to the car dealership where he apparently sold his car. He was last seen, by anyone we've talked to, hitchhiking on a feeder ramp to the north Tri-State Tollway."

"Well, that's a relief, at least," Lyssa said, letting out a long breath she had held in since Margo had begun. "It sounds like you've really been working hard."

"We've got a lot more than that," Wally said, "but on the other hand, we have nothing."

"It sounds like you've made some progress," Lyssa said. "I know more than I did yesterday."

"Well, yeah, but all we've done is disprove your contention that he was kidnapped or forced out of town."

"We haven't really proved the latter, Wally," Margo said.

He nodded. "I s'pose not. But you have to admit it appears he left on his own, under his own initiative, and with his own plan and schedule."

Margo agreed, then filled in Lyssa on what we'd learned at Faslund Paper. "My, you *have* been busy," Lyssa said. "I feel better already."

"But there's so much more we need to know about Byron if we're going to find him," Margo said. "Things that I'm afraid only you can tell us. He was so private with his friends that they have been able to do little but confirm the fact that he was private."

Lyssa sighed. "Maybe Mr. Walsh will be able to give you some more, but I don't know how talkative he'll be."

"You've met him?"

"Well, no. But Byron never said much about their conversations, so I just don't know whether maybe he'll be just as private as Byron."

"Does it bother you that the two people you put us onto were not aware of your relationship with Byron? Not even your name?"

"Not really," she said, weakly and unconvincingly. "You said yourself he was a very private person."

"But even private people brag about their loved ones," Margo said. "Or was your relationship not quite as important to him as it was to you?"

Lyssa stared at her. "What are you saying?"

"I'm not saying anything. I'm asking."

"You're suggesting something."

"Maybe I am," Margo admitted. "Is it true?"

"Are you working for me or against me?" Lyssa asked, her eyes moist.

"Did Byron Huttmann ever ask you to marry him?" Margo pressed.

"Not really," Lyssa said, "but—"

"Did he or didn't he?" Margo said, but Wally jumped in.

"Ah, Margo, listen," he said, "I'm among the best in badgering a suspect, but Miss Jack here has a point. She's not a suspect."

"I know, Wally," Margo said, "and Lyssa, I'm not trying to be mean, really I'm not, but we're chasing a shadow. Nobody he knows knows you, yet you say you were his almost-fiancée."

"We talked about marriage."

"Lots of people talk about marriage. Did he talk about your being his wife?"

"Yes."

"He did?"

"Yes."

"Tell me about it."

"One night he just opened up. We had been dating for a couple of months and had argued about church and Christianity for hours on end. He got kind of emotional and said I was the only girl he had ever loved, the only one he even thought of loving. He said he had seriously considered asking me to be his wife and that someday he probably would."

"Would—?"

"Would ask me."

"And what did you say?"

"I didn't say anything. I was speechless. He had never declared himself before, and it was what I'd been waiting for."

"But just a minute," I said. "Was this in the heat of an argument?"

"Well, yes."

60

"About your faith?"

"Yes."

"Then did he finish his point?"

"Sort of."

"How?"

"By saying that it could never work the way we were. That he would not marry someone who didn't agree with him on the most important, most basic things in life."

"There, you see?" Margo said. "It's just as we thought. You wouldn't change for him, and it was enough to send him packing."

"Well, actually, that night I told him I *would* change. I told him I had had no idea how he felt about me, but that I felt the same about him and that no argument about religion should stand in our way."

"How did he react to that?"

"Totally unpredictably," she said.

"Not to me," Margo said. "I'll bet he didn't want any part of it."

Lyssa looked puzzled. "Exactly right," she said. "But I've never known why."

"Even *I* know that," Wally said. "If this guy is for real, and from everything we can gather he is, the last thing he would want would be for you to change just to win him."

"What does he care why I change, as long as I change?"

"Just like with everything else in life," Wally said, "genuineness is determined by motive."

"How could he know my motive?"

"It was probably written all over you," Wally said. "It still is."

Lyssa stood and moved to the window, and with her back to us she spoke softly. We had to strain to catch

61

what she said. "You guys are like mind-readers," she said. "He questioned my motives, lectured me a little, gave me his basic sermon, and pretty much told me that he would be able to tell when and if I was for real about this."

"Did that offend you?" I asked.

"Not in the least," she said without turning around. "He had a way of saying it so lovingly and so truthfully that no one could be offended. I didn't agree with him, didn't think he was right — if I had I would have been terribly depressed. But I was certain of one thing: Byron believed it with all his heart, and I was afraid I could never convince him unless I really did change for real."

"You know you don't have to change, Lyssa," I said. "You come to God the way you are and He changes you."

"Mr. Spence," she said wearily, turning to face me now, "I know the whole story, all right? I mean I've heard it all a million times. I probably know it better than you do. I know how easy it is, I know what it means, I know my part, I know God's part, I know, I know, I know."

I held up both hands in surrender. "I'm sorry," I said.

"Don't be," she said. "I just wanted you to save your breath."

Wally stood and thrust his hands deep into his pockets. "Would you say this was a turning point in your relationship?"

"I sure would."

"And when did this take place?"

"About two months ago."

"How would you describe your relationship since then?"

62

"Strained."

"Still dating?"

"Oh, yes. Steadily."

"Really?"

"Sure, we were in love."

"He ever tell you that again?"

"No."

"You ever talk marriage again?"

"No."

"Did you talk about breaking up?"

"*I* didn't."

"Did he?"

She hung her head and nodded.

"Then why," Wally asked gently, "did you lead us to believe that the man was a few days from buying you a ring so you could announce, as you put it?"

She was crying. "I was just hoping, I guess. I still don't believe he disappeared because of me. He never backed down from our arguments, never gave up, kept asking me out."

"That *is* significant," Margo admitted.

"I thought so," Lyssa said.

Margo embraced her. "You're a special person," she said. "We want to help you and we don't mean to hassle you. We just need to know so much if we're going to find Byron." Lyssa stiffened, as if not entirely convinced, but Margo didn't back off. She continued: "I have to admit I'm becoming more and more convinced that you're not going to like what we find out about why he left."

"Why?"

"It just had to have something to do with you."

"But why no warning?"

"Are you sure there was none? Or weren't you listening?"

Lyssa shook her head, then rested it on Margo's shoulder. "I don't know," she said. "But I sure want you to stick with this and find out for me. I can't stand not knowing."

After Lyssa left that night, Wally was unusually quiet and pensive. "You thinking about something, chief?" I asked.

He just grunted.

"Where are we on this thing, Wal?" Margo tried.

Still nothing.

"Are you mad at me, Wally?" she asked. "Did I blow it tonight?"

"I've seen you better," he said. "But nah, that's not it."

"I'm sorry I was so blunt," Margo said, "but this one really has me frustrated. We've got a guy out there hitchhiking with a pocket full of severance pay and car money, and all we know is he drove a rented truck about three hundred miles. There are more than a few people inside that radius."

We all nodded and stared at the floor, slowly turning back and forth in our swivel chairs. "Something's on your mind, Wally," I said.

"How can you tell?" he said.

"Because usually you're up and around and summarizing and plotting and eager to get on with it." I stood and imitated his waddling gait and gruff voice. "OK kids, let's get some sleep and hit it tomorrow. Let's close in on this guy."

Margo laughed, but Wally just smiled. He stood and moved slowly toward his office. At the door he turned and said, "What do you make of this girl?"

We thought a moment. "Troubled," Margo said.

"Yeah," Wally agreed.

64

"Pretty," I said, stating the inappropriate and unrelated obvious in a vain attempt to be funny. Neither responded with so much as a smile. "Seriously," I said, "I would agree with troubled."

"Smart move," Wally said, turning toward his door again. He stopped and turned back. "What I meant was," he said, "what do you make of the fact that she says she knows the whole story, about God and everything?"

"She does know it, apparently," Margo said. "She's had some good tutoring."

"But it didn't work. How does somebody get the whole picture, know the whole thing, like she said, and not buy into it?"

We sat silent, letting him answer his own question. He kept talking. "I mean, once ol' Earl Haymeyer got the picture, even before he had acted on it himself, he was telling me all about it. I've found myself wanting to do the same with this girl. But she *knows* it all! She knows it all and she's got more than enough reasons, and, and—ah, I don't know."

Uncharacteristically, Wally was standing still, staring at the floor. "Wally," Margo said quietly, "are you saying that someone who sees the whole picture of God's love could not resist it for long?"

He nodded.

"Is that what's troubling you, Wal? Does she remind you of you?"

He nodded again. "Sort of," he said, hardly audible. "But I don't think I'll ever tell anybody I don't want to hear it again, just because I know it all."

"Would you like to hear it again tonight, before you go home?" Margo asked.

"Maybe," he said shuffling over to the desk near her and resting his bulk on the top. "Just one more time to make sure I have it all straight. I still don't want you to push me into anything," he added. "I'll do this on my own."

"Of course," Margo said. And she told him again what we had told him so many times before, about how God wanted to establish a relationship with him, with Walvoord Feinberg Festschrift.

And that night at home, we prayed as never before that God would work in his life. That maybe God would use even the rebellion of Lyssa Jack to bring Wally Festschrift to Himself.

Chapter Eight

"It's no wonder the cops wouldn't take this case," I said miserably Thursday morning as Margo and I drove south on Glencoe Road until just before it became Green Bay Road again. "We shouldn't have taken it either."

We headed east on Tower to Sheridan Road and turned south again through Wilmette and into Kenilworth.

"Why so grumpy this morning?" Margo said. "I didn't realize you were in a bad mood."

"I'm not. I'm just starting to see this case for what it is. A ruse."

"You really think so? You think she's putting us on, that she knows where he is?"

"I don't know about that," I said, "but when we find the guy, there's going to be little mystery in it. If he drove the truck at least a hundred and twenty miles from his new apartment to the rental place and sold his car, of course he's not going to pay a cabbie to take him back to his new apartment."

"But why wouldn't he have a friend take him to his new place? He didn't even let anyone help him."

"That *is* baffling. But I can't imagine it's worth the time and effort of three private investigators."

"I think it's fascinating, Philip. For once there's no

foul play, no murder, no mayhem. Just an interesting puzzle. There's going to be one or two very disappointed people, not the least of which will likely be our client, but I'm dying to know where we're going to find this guy."

"We're going to find him in a new apartment, somewhere north of Chicago and south of Milwaukee, entertaining offers from big corporations. His stubborn girl friend spurred an early mid-life crisis, and he decided it was time for a big career move."

"That's it, you think?" Margo said.

"Yup. That's it."

"How boring."

"Thanks a lot."

"I didn't mean you, sweetheart," she said. "Just your theory."

"You know I'm right."

"Let's say I'm afraid you're right. Still, I'm intrigued, and I'm glad Lyssa came to us with her problem. How else would I get to see a place like this?"

We pulled into a long, winding drive that led to a circular turnaround in front of a mansion like I had never seen before, except in pictures. The long, reddish stone building had a tower on each end, and I realized we had likely been watched from the time we entered the gate.

Two men in business suits emerged from the house as I stopped the car. "Just leave it running, if you will, Mr. Spence," the older said as he opened the door for Margo. "Claude will park it for you, sir. Right this way, please. Mr. Walsh is waiting for you."

As I moved out from behind the wheel, Claude slid in, adjusted the seat, and pulled away. Margo and I glanced at each other as we followed the butler up the steps and into the marble-floored foyer with a vaulted ceiling that went three stories to a magnificent skylight.

A handsome woman in her mid-forties approached from the other end of the hall and it was clear that she would be less formal, though no less dignified. "Mr. and Mrs. Spence, ma'am," the butler said, taking our coats and disappearing behind us.

"Thank you, Albert," she said cheerily, extending a hand to each of us and flashing a toothy smile. "Shirley Walsh," she said. "It's nice to meet both of you. I'll take you to Father."

We followed her until the marble turned to parquet, then deep pile carpeting. She stopped before a heavy wood door that stood slightly ajar and leaned her ear to it. She knocked loudly twice.

"Yes," came the pleasant voice from within.

"Mr. and Mrs. Spence from the EH Detective Agency, Father," she said, opening the door.

"Thank you, Shirley," Mr. Walsh said with a certain finality, which we assumed meant that she could leave us. Which she did.

Collin J. Walsh was a tall, white-haired man, trim but with a big barrel chest. He was dressed in a powder blue three-piece suit which would have looked out of place in early November, except that it was clearly a blend of heavy, natural wool.

His suit was buttoned, and he looked as if he were ready for a ride to work. I almost offered. He was a pleasant-looking, thin-lipped grandfatherly sort, except that his bearing was straight and formal and more than a little intimidating.

His den was done in cherry wood, and he offered us comfortable chairs at the front of his huge desk. He unbuttoned his suitcoat and sat on the edge of his high-backed chair, leaning forward and resting his elbows on the desktop and folding his hands, fingers intertwined.

"Detectives you say, huh?" he began. We nodded, smiling. "And you want to find young Huttmann. I dare say if he doesn't want to be found, you won't find him."

"Does he not want to be found?" I asked.

"What makes you think I would know?"

"Every person we talk to says you two are close."

He stared at us. "Every person, meaning whom?"

"People who are acquainted with you both."

"Faslund employees, no doubt. They think I don't know what goes on, that I'm not aware of their games. I've told By more than once that I don't care what they think or say and that he shouldn't either. I'm not saying I don't care about them in relation to their work, you understand. It's the—what shall we call it?—the extracurricular activity."

That made him smile, and we followed suit.

"But do you know where he is?" Margo asked. "I'm not asking you to tell us if he's asked you not to. I'm just curious to know if you know."

Walsh smiled slightly. "Why?"

"It will confirm what we've learned about your relationship."

"What do you care about our relationship?"

Margo was a bit taken aback. "Well, I, uh, we don't, ah, care that much about it as much as we care to determine the credibility of our sources."

"And if they were right about our relationship, you could trust whatever else they might have told you."

We nodded.

"Uh-huh," he said, swiveling in his chair to look out

70

the window. We could see our car parked next to a huge garage, and in the distance, workmen fixing up one of the buildings on the property.

"I've been very close to the boy," he said suddenly, swinging back around to face us. He took off his coat as he spoke, rolled up his sleeves, and loosened his tie. Our cue, I assumed, that he was not in a hurry and not reluctant to talk about one of his favorite subjects.

He looked past me and seemed to be staring at the wall beyond, almost as if reading cue cards. "I remember the day the recruiter who had landed Byron brought him to my office. It was Byron's first week at the office, or first month, I don't know. I may have been away when he first started.

"But that's a tradition of ours. Let the recruiter show off his find. Well, they all come in with the same pitch, telling me they've found the brightest stars of the future for the company. I've seen a lot of them come and go. I've seen a lot of good ones too. But none like young Huttmann. Seems like yesterday."

"You could tell he was a winner from the start?"

"Oh, no, no one can do that, except a recruiter, you know? And they're nine times out of ten wrong themselves!" He smiled. "No, he was a memorable kid, but I made no predictions at the time."

"What was so memorable about him?" Margo asked.

"Well, there was no baloney. He didn't try to impress me like so many of them do."

"And you liked that? I would think you'd want a trainee to be concerned about impressing the boss."

"Oh, well, I don't like the ones who try to get too familiar or critical or blunt right off the bat. But that wasn't him. He was just honest enough to say that he hadn't been with us long enough to know how well he

71

liked it, but also that liking it had little to do with what he hoped to learn and contribute as soon as he was able. I liked that. Fresh approach. New way of saying it."

"Did you encourage him?" I asked.

"Yes. Yes, I did. I told him that with an attitude like that, not only would he learn and contribute, but he *would* also like Faslund. And I believe he did."

"You're not sure?"

"Yes, I'm sure. I shouldn't have said it that way. He did for sure. And we liked him. Who wants to find him?"

"His girl friend."

"Which one?"

"He had more than one?"

Mr. Walsh folded his arms and sat back, a smile playing at his lips. "Just testing you," he said. "Give me one of her names, and I'll give you the other."

The game seemed out of character for him, but then we had had him pigeon-holed since we'd rolled through the gate. "Jack," I said.

"Lyssa," he said, almost simultaneously. "Where's she getting the money for private detectives?"

"We didn't ask," I said.

"But you took the first payment up front, didn't you?"

His attack seemed unwarranted. "We don't discuss our business arrangements," I said, trying not to sound cold. I noted from his color that I had not succeeded, so I decided to plunge ahead. "I have to think you know where Byron is, because if you didn't you'd be as worried as Lyssa Jack."

He smiled with respect and nodded. "Maybe more so," he said.

"Did you want to finish your story about your

relationship with him?" Margo suggested, ever sensitive.

The faraway look returned almost immediately. "He was athletic. Looked it, acted it, was it. Good golfer, did you know that? Surely you came across that."

We hadn't, but he didn't really wait for an answer anyway. "He was a superstar in the office, and I don't mean in sports. His first promotion didn't have anything to do with me. I mean, none of them did, but there wasn't even any suspicion surrounding the first one."

I wanted to ask him about the talk surrounding the rest of them, but I didn't want to interrupt.

"Byron impressed his superiors by doing his homework, asking good questions, deferring to authority without becoming a yes man. He worked well with other departments. Very quickly established himself as a rising star but was seemingly selfless. Humble. Never talked about himself. Reminded me so much of Paul."

He fell silent. His eyes reddened. Neither of us could ask who Paul was. We both knew. We waited.

"Paul was my son," he managed. "I lost him to a drunk driver the night of his high school graduation in nineteen seventy."

He didn't speak for several seconds. "Did Byron and your son look alike, Mr. Walsh?" Margo asked.

He shook his head. "Didn't act alike either. Oh, Paul was a good enough kid, but he was a rebel like so many. *He* was the drunk driver, by the way. I always refer to him that way when I talk about the accident. It's because I have never forgiven the drunk driver part of him for taking the other part of him from me."

"Why did Byron remind you so much of him?" Margo asked.

"I don't know," he said. "Other than that they were

73

close in age. I suppose Byron is everything I had hoped Paul would become. And I believe deep down he would have someday, in spite of the stage he was going through."

"When did you become friends with Byron?"

The old man chuckled, still staring in the distance. "When he humiliated me on the golf course. Indian Hill. It was a company outing. We were paired off. I always asked to be in a foursome with the best player in the company. Usually they sandbag just enough to let me beat them. I still shoot in the high eighties, of which I'm quite proud.

"But this day, Byron Huttmann was unconscious on the course. I believe he shot par. Hardly anyone ever does that at Indian Hill. But all the way, he kept apologizing for his deadly shooting. He kept insisting that he was playing way over his head. That breaking eighty was the best he had ever done. I kept telling him to go for it and quit feeling badly about it. In truth, he brought my game up. Seems I was in the mid-eighties that day, but he smoked me. By more than a dozen strokes. Finished with two eagles. Just dynamite."

"And that started your relationship?" Margo asked, not quite understanding it all and letting it show in her tone of voice.

"Oh, my, no, it wasn't the golf," Walsh said, looking patiently at her. "It was the mistake he made on purpose to give me the round. It was a stroke of genius, pardon the pun. The boy was too competitive and dedicated to blow a shot, but he wasn't above messing up his score card."

"I don't understand," Margo said.

"Well, he somehow got off the track and started

marking his score for each hole on the wrong line. I think it happened on the thirteenth or fourteenth hole where it was obvious he was going to have a fantastic round. He shot fours on three holes in a row, but he claimed he forgot he had already written one and wound up writing it twice, so when he shot the three at seventeen, he marked it for eighteen and conceded the round to me because of his invalid score card."

Walsh smiled at the memory of it.

"Did you let him get away with it?" I asked.

"Oh, no," he said, adding an epithet. "I chided him for doing it on purpose, and he couldn't hide a grin, though I never got him to admit it. I told everyone about his score, and why wouldn't I? I don't need to win every year, though I usually do. Or did, until Byron came along. Good golfing name, you know, Byron."

"Yes," I said.

"No," Margo said.

Walsh chuckled again. "You know that boy tried to find reasons not to go golfing with me after that. I had to make it a directive."

"You did, really?" I said.

"Absolutely."

"You ever beat him?"

"I have all the scores right here," he said, digging in a drawer. "I beat him once. But I'm convinced he let me. Here, let me show you on the card."

Sure enough, Byron Huttman's game had seemingly fallen apart over the last three holes. He averaged two more shots per hole than he had for the first fifteen and lost the match by two.

When I looked up, Mr. Walsh was grinning at me,

brows raised, as if stifling a belly laugh. "Tell me it isn't obvious, huh? Hey, tell me! Huh?"

I nodded and smiled. He shoved the card under Margo's nose and spent several minutes explaining it to her. "Just like miniature golf," she said.

He was crestfallen, as any golfing addict would have been. "Sort of," he mumbled.

Chapter Nine

If there was one thing of which I was certain that afternoon, it was that Faslund President Collin J. Walsh knew precisely where we could find Byron Huttmann.

The old man almost gleefully showed us scorecards, photographs, and scrapbooks. We were shocked, really, to realize that the two had spent so much time together. Even the people who thought they knew all about the relationship had not had a hint of the sheer hours the two had spent on the golf course, camping, fishing, even vacationing.

"Did your daughter accompany you on the vacations?" Margo asked, admiring his photographs taken at the Princess Hotel in Bermuda.

Walsh returned from his reverie and slowly looked up at her. "Yes, she did," he said. "And I know what you're driving at."

"I'm not driving at anything, really——"

"Oh, it's all right, a natural question. With my wife, Maxine—there, look at that fish Maxie caught; caught it herself—Byron might have felt like a fifth wheel. And I use Shirley so much, you know, for business. I'm never really away from the business, of course. But people make assumptions, yes. They think maybe By and Shirley room together or are married or something or another. But it just isn't the case. They appreciate and enjoy each other, but there's nothing there, improper or otherwise. They don't date, they don't spend time alone together. They just know each other in our foursome. She's considerably older than he is, you know."

"But certainly not an unattractive woman," I said.

Walsh swore. "Of course not. She's a beautiful woman."

I wouldn't have gone that far, but neither would I have been surprised to learn that Byron Huttmann had fallen for her on one of the Walsh trips.

Soon Walsh began glancing at his watch every few minutes. "Late for work?" I asked.

"I'm *at* work," he said, not unkindly. "I'm just not at the office."

"We won't keep you," I said. "If there's anything, anything at all you can tell us that might help us locate Mr. Huttmann—"

"I have a better idea," he said. "Why don't I tell you that he's fine and better off not disturbed?"

"That's what we should tell our client?" I said, regretting it as soon as it came out of my mouth. "I mean, she'll never buy it."

"Is that all you care about?" he said, not amused. "What she'll buy? She expecting more for her money? I don't care what you tell your client. I've told you all I'm going to tell you."

"I'm sorry," I said. "I didn't mean that the way it sounded."

"You meant it just the way you said it."

Now I was angry. I didn't care how rich and important and powerful he was or thought he was; he couldn't tell me what I meant.

"I did not," I said, reddening and clearly alarming

78

Margo. "And I ought to know. Even if you're a mind reader, you don't know my thoughts better than I do."

Then I felt foolish because I had nowhere to go with my argument. He glared at me, sizing me up as if wondering why he was wasting his time.

"Nice try," he said with disgust. "If I thought you cared about Byron, it might be a different story. But you're here for the same reason Lyssa Jack has been nosing around. You want something. For you it's enough to show that you've earned your fee. For her, who knows what it is?"

"Lyssa Jack's been nosing around here?" Margo asked, ignoring his real point.

The question caught him off guard. "Well, not here but at the office. You must know that."

"What do *you* think she wants, Mr. Walsh?" I asked, careful to address him with respect to show that I didn't want to continue the verbal tussle.

By now he was rearranging himself, rolling down and buttoning his sleeves, buttoning his top button and tightening his tie, slipping on his suitcoat, and heading for his overcoat draped over a chair.

"Who knows what she wants?" he said. "Not even Byron could ever figure that out. They never agreed on religion. I don't suppose she's told you that. And when he saw that she would never change her mind, he gave up on her. That's what I think. He would never admit it. It's what I wanted."

"Were you jealous of her?" Margo tried, slowing him down.

He paused with his coat over his arm and stared at her, as if with respect. "I searched myself about that," he said. "I knew marriage would have monopolized his time, and I had grown to love him as a son. But when I began hoping nothing would come of this girl, I had to examine my motives. I came to the conclusion that I wanted more for him. A better woman. I wanted him to marry well. I hoped for more class for him, but I wanted him to have at least what he wanted, and that would have been someone who agreed with him in his deepest beliefs."

"Did you?" Margo asked.

Collin Walsh was suddenly emotional. It was as if he couldn't speak. He pressed his lips together to keep them from trembling, then he bit his bottom lip. He licked his lips and pressed them together again, and his breathing became shallow. "Let me say this," he managed huskily. "We talked about it for hours and hours and, no, I never once truly believed it was all as simple as Byron said it was. I blamed it on his conservative upbringing, but I grew to see that he truly believed.

"I'm a religious man. I pray. I'm in church at least twice a month. I believe in God. But I'm not born again, and I don't know if heaven is a real place. I don't believe there's a hell, that a loving God would create a place like that. I hate to admit it, but when Byron told me how heartsick he was over this Lyssa's not agreeing with him on that, I couldn't bring myself to tell him that I pretty much agreed with her."

"But it bothers you," Margo said gently.

He cocked his head as if to say she could assume whatever she wanted.

"There's something we must tell you, Mr. Walsh," she said quickly. "If you could give us just a few more minutes."

He didn't even look at his watch. He immediately sat in the chair that had held his coat, which he now folded in his lap. So, he had not really been in a hurry; he was just ready to exit the conversation. He raised his chin and stared blankly at Margo, as if waiting for her to begin.

"I want to tell you how we have come to care about Byron," she said.

He sighed and rolled his eyes, and I knew he was asking himself why he had consented to more talk.

"It's true," she added. "Let me explain. We share Byron's, ah, religious beliefs, though my guess is that he at one time or another explained to you that his faith should not really be considered a religion. It's a —"

"Person, yes. Yes, he did. So Lyssa came to you because she figured you'd be sympathetic with him? I don't get it."

"Oh, no, just the opposite," Margo said. "It was strictly coincidental that we were Christians too, but it did allow us to empathize and to understand what they had been arguing about."

He held up his hands. "So?" he said. "That's it? That's what you wanted more time to tell me?"

"No sir," she said, undaunted. "I'm trying to tell you that though we've never met the man, we feel like we know him. We have talked to co-workers, bosses, friends, everyone but family. They've given us a picture of a man who's — yes, maybe a little too good to be true — but who's someone we want to know. Someone we would like. Someone we would identify with. I don't usually make a practice of talking about someone behind her back, however, I must say, and I think Philip would agree, that from everything we've learned, we share your view of Byron and we're less impressed with Lyssa."

Mr. Walsh pretended to be bored or confused, but I could tell from the look deep in his eyes that he was neither. "So, what are you trying to say?" he asked.

"That we do care about Byron," she said. "That for many reasons other than our client and our fees, we want to know where he is, to be sure he's all right, to meet him, to get to know him."

Walsh stood and pulled on his coat. "I can help you with the first two," he said. "Yes, I know where he is. He's all right. You'll not be meeting him or getting to know him."

"But why?" Margo asked.

"Because that's the way he wants it."

"He knows about us?"

"I'd rather not talk about it."

"You're in constant communication with him then."

"Shall we say frequent, not constant."

"Is he still on the payroll of Faslund Paper?" I asked.

He shook his head and then caught himself. "Uh, yes, of course, during the next several months, as you learned at the office."

"But you have the power to keep him on the payroll," I pressed. "If for no other reason than your friendship."

"I wouldn't do that," he said coldly.

"Who paid for the outings, the trips?"

"Byron offered."

"But you never accepted."

He ignored my remark. "Byron refused to be kept on the payroll."

"You offered?"

"Yes, of course, I offered. All right? Anything more?"

"Just one thing," Margo said.

"You said that a few minutes ago, and I'm still here."

"I'm sorry. It's really the same issue. I just want to know if you believe us that we're personally interested in Byron Huttmann."

82

"I have no reason to doubt you."

"You don't sound like you mean that," she said.

"Don't I? I guess I don't. I already told you I thought you had ulterior motives. If you say you don't, fine then, you don't. You're believable enough. But I'm not turning Byron over to you either because you have a client with an interest in him or because of your religious curiosity."

"You're saying he left of his own volition, and that he isn't seeking or accepting your help, and that he's all right?" Margo summarized.

"Most of that is correct, yes."

"Can you tell me what part of it is incorrect?"

"No."

"Can I assume something?" I broke in. "Can I assume that you tried to talk Byron out of all this, whatever it is?"

"You may assume that, yes. My wish is that he would have stayed with the company, stayed my friend and companion, stayed just exactly the way he was."

"He's changed?"

"I'm through talking. Really. I've said too much already. I've said much more than Byron would be pleased with."

"Can you tell us who else knows where Byron is and what's going on?"

"No one that I know. That's the way he wants it."

"Do you mind if we talk to your wife and daughter?"

"Not at all," he said, excusing himself and opening the door. He paused only briefly, half turned, and said, "Now, you'll forgive me, but I must go." He left and shut the door.

I looked at Margo. "I'm more confused than ever," I said.

"Me too," she said.

83

And Collin Walsh reappeared. "In fact," he said, "you'll get a real kick out of Shirley. Now, she won't be able to tell you anything about Byron, of course, but she bought his whole package, lock, stock, and barrel."

"His whole package?"

"Yeah! The religious bit."

Chapter Ten

Margo and I stood silently in the cavernous Walsh study, wondering if we should venture out. Who knew where Albert had left our coats, or whether we were even allowed unescorted passage through such an estate?

The door swung open and the gregarious, almost vivacious, dark-haired Shirley Walsh flashed that smile. "I guess we need our coats," Margo said.

Shirley Walsh's smile faded into a puzzled look. "Well, Father said you wanted to talk to me," she said.

"Oh, we'd love to, yes," I said.

"Then, please, come to my office. This one is so cold."

"I found it comfortable," Margo said as we followed her down the hall.

"Oh, I don't mean the temperature," she said. "It's just so stiff and formal. So macho."

"But I understand you're in charge of that sort of thing around here," Margo said. "The decorating, I mean."

"I am, but of course Father is the boss. If he wants a den full of over-sized furniture and appointments, that's what I have made for him. At least I worked in plenty of warm wood, wouldn't you say?" We both nodded and smiled.

At the end of the hall near the stairs, Albert hurried toward us with our coats. "I'll fetch your car in Claude's absence," he said, Claude having apparently driven Mr. Walsh to work.

"It'll be just a little while, Albert, thank you," Miss Walsh said. "The Spences will be with me in my office, and you'll be in charge of the house. Please, no interruptions except for emergencies."

"Very good, ma'am," he said with a slight bow and trucked off again with our coats.

Shirley's office was in the north tower of the main residence with a wide, curved window overlooking the front expanse of the estate. Indeed, she could have seen us pull in the drive, just as we suspected.

Her wood furniture was black with delicate oriental art painted on several pieces. And her desk was not really a desk but rather an ornate thin-legged table set off by colorful wall hangings and charcoal sketches.

It was difficult to not just gawk at everything, and we were both speechless. It was the type of room that if one area had been done to excess, it would have spoiled everything. But with the understated emphasis on Asian art and fresh flowers, the room was perfect, homey, informal, inviting.

She directed us to a fluffy loveseat and sat across from us in a floral winged-back chair. A tiny table between us had butterfly wings imbedded in a thick lamination. Shirley, still smiling, crossed her legs, folded her arms, and asked how she could help us. We would agree later that her body language betrayed her unwillingness to talk.

I decided to take a direct, blunt approach and see how open she would be to really help us. I think my first question even startled Margo. "Would you agree with me," I said, "that your father is naive to think that Paul would have ever become what Byron apparently is?"

Again the smile faded and a puzzled squint replaced it. When Shirley did manage to speak, it was if she had forgotten to breathe first. "You mean that Paul wasn't capable?" she said.

"No, not that he wasn't capable. But that he didn't seem the type to suddenly turn himself around. From what I've heard of him, he seems to have been a very troubled young man, deeply troubled. It's as if his rebellion was just evidence of a deeper problem he had with his upbringing, his father's life-style. Am I right?"

"I have no idea," Shirley said, almost coldly. "I've really never thought about it. I'll concede that, in his memory, Father may have Paul overrated. He blamed everything on the alcohol, rather than blaming the alcohol on the inconsistency of this life-style. Past that, I'm not qualified to comment. You see, I'm part of this life-style. It hasn't eluded me that we're privileged, and that we probably don't deserve what we have."

"Do you know what you have in relation to others?" I asked.

"I don't want to get off on a philosophical discussion of the class system," she said, "but yes, I'm aware that not everyone in this town has the size staff we have."

"Are you aware how rare it is that a family has a staff at all? Do you have any idea the percentage of American families who have no help at all?"

"Yes, I think I do. Do you want me to feel guilty because we can afford this life-style? Father could feel guilty because he gives so little to charity. And I feel badly about how little I used to give, but I've tried to make up for that. And we're at ease with our life-style. We don't lord it over anyone."

"Why was your brother so eager to dissociate himself from the family then?"

"I don't know what you're driving at, and I don't know either how this is going to help us — I mean you — find By. Byron. Mr. Huttmann. Regardless, I'll answer. Paul never once tried to dissociate himself from us. On the contrary, he drove his father's sports car. Killed himself in it. He used his father's credit cards. He threw a lot of parties here. He may have had a deep-seated problem with his station in life, but he wasn't about to cash it in. He stayed in his father's good graces enough to get whatever he wanted whenever he wanted it. I don't think father has ever forgiven himself for that. My sister and I were not raised that way."

Margo was looking at me, trying to silently convey the fact that she thought we should get to the topic at hand. I knew we should too, but I had wanted to get a better bead on Shirley Walsh, and I thought I had, but I didn't know where to go with it now. It was significant to me that while Shirley was clearly annoyed at my questioning and had indicated that she wanted to move on to something else, she had not been bothered enough to ask us to leave.

In fact, she seemed willing to bear with me as long as possible until we got onto the subject she was most interested in. I could have been wrong, but I was under the impression that she wanted to talk about Byron Huttmann.

"Let's talk about Byron," I said, and she immediately unfolded her arms, uncrossed her legs, sat forward daintily, and entwined her fingers in her lap. Without waiting for a specific question, she began.

"I met him in the spring of nineteen seventy-six when father invited him up to the house after the annual company golf outing. Father likes to play with whoever is the best player in the company, even though the outing is really for Faslund's most prized clients. Of course the clients never have anyone who can compete with Father. He played in several pro-am tournaments in the fifties and sixties, and he had been beaten only once before by anyone in the company. I think he had been ill or had injured his leg or something. Still lost by only a few strokes. Nino Bernardini beat him, but he regretted it."

"Your father didn't like that?"

"Oh, no, that wasn't it! He got a kick out of it, but the other executives made Nino fear for his life, his job, his future. It was hilarious. In subsequent years, Father thinks Nino let him win several times. He always felt Nino was the better golfer. He would hear of Nino's better scores during the year, but Father always beat him at the annual bash. He hated that. He loved competition more than anything. I think that's why he loved Byron so much."

"But didn't Byron sandbag against your father too? It's obvious from the scorecards."

"Oh, he showed you those too?" she said, genuinely surprised and maybe impressed that her father had felt that free that quickly with us. "Yes, well, he knew Byron was, ah, sandbagging, as you call it, but it always impressed Father how deftly By did it. You know what I mean?"

We nodded. "Tell us about your relationship with Byron," Margo said.

Shirley blushed. "We didn't have a relationship, actually. I mean we never dated each other or liked each other or anything. I mean, well, we liked each other, you know, but not in a relationship sense. We weren't interested in each other in a romantic way, you know."

I could tell Margo was amused, though she hid her smile. She had asked a question that had flustered this woman, and Margo didn't want to let up. She pressed for more detail.

"You didn't like him, you mean? He surely was enamored with you early on, right?"

"Oh, I don't think so. Who told you that? Father didn't tell you that, did he?"

"No, I was just thinking that a young man on the rise in your father's corporation, single, from humble beginnings, would have to be impressed with a beautiful, only slightly older woman who's well-to-do, well read, well traveled."

"Oh, no, I don't know. We always enjoyed chatting, but no, I don't think he was ever, um—how did you say it?—enamored with me. No."

"Were you of him?"

"Enamored? Oh, I, uh, no. No, I wouldn't say that. No. Not enamored."

"Did you ever develop a crush on him?" Margo said with a twinkle.

A smile threatened to force its way to Shirley's mouth. "Oh, well, he was, and is, an impressive young man. I liked him immediately, from the minute I first laid eyes—well, since I first met him."

"We've never met him," Margo said, "but we feel as if we know him. He almost seems too good to be true. Did you find him that way?"

"Oh yes, he *is* too good to be true. No one I've ever met could be that true, that consistent, that good on his own. Not even Byron."

"Then he's not all he's cracked up to be?" I asked, pretending not to know what she was getting at.

"Oh, yes, he is. He's just not that way on his own. No one could be. He's human like everyone else."

90

"Then what is it?" Margo asked, playing along with me.

"I asked him the same thing once. We were in Gulf Shores, Louisiana, where Daddy, uh, Father has a boat."

"You had some time alone with him?"

"Occasionally. We liked to go shopping together here and there, sometimes in the early afternoon when father was napping or in the early evening after dinner. Mother might go with us, might not. If she did, she liked to go off on her own for an hour or so, and we would get chances to talk. We became quite good friends, actually."

"Was your mother trying to do some matchmaking?"

"Not at all. She respected and admired By very much, but she warned me once about becoming attached to him. She felt I would never be happy with a younger man, and also a man who—while he had a great future and would undoubtedly do very well for himself and his family—was new to money and would never be totally comfortable with the kind of life-style I had become accustomed to."

"Was she right?"

"I never gave it a thought?"

"You *were* interested then?"

"I didn't say that. I just meant that her logic, or lack of it, would never have influenced me in relation to Byron."

A smile was playing at Margo's lips again. I could tell she felt she had Shirley on the ropes, that with a little more time she could ferret out some admission of more of an emotional tie between them. Maybe it was only from Shirley's side. Maybe Byron never felt the same. But it seemed clear that Shirley had indeed been interested in Byron Huttmann. More than she was willing to let on.

"So you asked him what made him different, is that it?"

"Not exactly," Shirley said. "I was asking him what it was he and Father had been discussing all afternoon that had seemed to upset father so much. He told me it was about his faith in Christ."

She smiled at the thought of it and grew silent. When she spoke again she reminded us of how her father had reminisced, looking into the distance, almost ignoring us, as if she were back in Gulf Shores.

"The four of us had walked up and down the beach. We had sunbathed, swam, played games. We were hot and tired. More than tired. We were exhausted. Our hair had been bleached by the sun. We were bone weary, achy, sunburned.

"Father just wanted to rest after dinner. We had steak and lobster delivered to the boat. Mother and Byron and I dressed in light, loose-fitting clothes and sandals and strolled into town. Mother went off to shop, and By and I sat on a pier. The sunset was gorgeous.

"He was a bit troubled by the angry reaction he had received from Father, but Father had repeatedly told him that day, 'This won't affect our relationship, By, we just can't let it. But we're going to stand disagreed.'

"I told Byron that Father was serious, that they could stand disagreed without his holding a grudge and that By shouldn't worry about it. It would be all right. That kind of talk. But he told me that it wasn't his relationship to Father he was worried about, even though he cherished it. It was Father's relationship to God."

"How did you react to that?"

"I could hardly believe it. I knew Byron was a wonderful young man, but I also figured that he knew what kind of fortune he had fallen into. He had become like a son to the most important man in his life. His future was secure. My father adored him."

"Did you tell Byron that?"

"Yes, I did. I told him his view of God was interesting and that I appreciated his concern for my father, but I also told him my father was Christian and that maybe he should appreciate more the benefits of being my father's favorite person. 'You're like a son to him,' I told him. You know what he told me? He told me he had an earthly father that no one could substitute for and that he had a heavenly Father that even his own father couldn't measure up to. That's when I asked him if it was his religious beliefs that made him the way he was."

She chuckled at the memory. "He said he didn't know what he was, but that he hoped his faith permeated his life. I asked him if he didn't care what my father thought of him anymore. He said he cared very much, but that if becoming an enemy of my father would bring my father to Christ, he would be willing to become his enemy. I told him I didn't think that would be necessary; he said he hoped not, and then we got serious."

"You got serious?"

"Yes. I told him he'd better give me the straight dope on his faith. He began by telling me that he assumed I had the same outlook as my father. About the only thing I remember from that conversation was his explaining the difference between being Christian and being *a* Christian. Would you be offended if I explained it to you the way he explained it to me?"

"Not at all," Margo said. "But I thought you didn't remember anything else about that conversation."

"That's true. But that conversation was continued every time we got together over the next two years. We picked up right where we left off in places as divergent as Bermuda and Sanibel Island. I was as eager to hear it as he was to tell it. And now I'm as eager to tell it as he was."

Chapter Eleven

Neither Margo nor I felt right about letting Shirley Walsh attempt to evangelize us. Margo handled it well.

"We want to hear your story," she said softly. "But we want to hear it a little differently than you might want to tell it."

"I don't understand."

"It's just that it sounds like you want to tell us what happened to you with the hope that we might see that the same could happen to us."

She looked surprised. "Well, that's exactly right. But—"

"We share your faith, Shirley."

"You do?" she said, many things making sense for her now for the first time. She let out a huge sigh, and her body seemed to lose its tension.

"We do," Margo said, leaning forward and reaching across to briefly take her hand. "We want to hear your story for that reason, not for any other. It might change the way you tell it if you know we understand."

"But how did you know?"

"Your father told us."

"But he doesn't—he isn't—"

"We know. But he knows what happened to you."

"He just thinks I—"

"Bought Byron's package."

"Exactly. That's what he thinks. He said that too?"
We nodded and she smiled. And she told us of a beautiful, miraculous story of how she moved from defensiveness to skepticism to curiosity. She told of hours' worth of conversations with Byron where she slowly turned from her father's view of religion and church to a Bible-based, Christ-centered perspective.

"But of course, that wasn't enough," she said. "I had to make a decision for myself. Byron made a major point of the fact that truly becoming a Christian was a transaction. At some point, he told me, I would have to do something on my own, independent of him or my father or my family or my church. I would have to receive Christ. It took me many months to get to the point where I felt I was ready, and when the time came I wasn't any more ready than I'd ever been, and all I could do was wonder why I had waited so long."

Shirley wept as she told the story of the night she prayed and told God that she believed in Him and received Christ. "Did Byron know?" Margo asked.

"No, that was the irony of it. I had become so dependent upon him for answers that I felt a little lost when he was away. I counted on him spending every other weekend or so with Father, but he was out of the country on business and I didn't know who to tell."

"Did you tell anyone?"

"Yes, I told my mother. She thought I'd gone stark raving mad. She accused me of being in love with Byron and doing it just to please him. She said she didn't know if she should call Father at the office or never tell him. I told her to do the latter."

"To never tell him? Why?"

"Because *I* wanted to tell him. I called him myself. He was very quiet, very reserved. I had a difficult time expressing myself, but he could tell I was serious, that it was not some lark. Of course, I was never the type to be faddish or a follower anyway, so he didn't worry about that. I think mostly it hit him close to home. He'll never admit it, unless he eventually comes to the same conclusions I did, but he may have felt Byron's persuasion closing in on him because of me. On the other hand, my conversion may have strengthened his resolve to fight it."

"What did he say?"

"Well, he took the tack of trying to defend his own form of Christianity. He advised me to be careful about thinking that this was any more important or better or even different from what happened at our own church every Sunday. I told him, 'Daddy, we haven't been in our own church two Sundays in a row for twenty years.' He ignored that, told me to quit calling him Daddy, and to just not get too carried away."

"Did that hurt you?"

"Not really, no. I expected it. It was all right. Of course, I *had* already gotten carried away, and he was just going to have to live with it. I couldn't wait to team up with Byron and go after Father."

"And did you do that?"

"Yes, but not successfully. But we haven't given up. That's one of the reasons I'm so curious to know where Byron is and what's happened."

"You really don't know?" I asked, figuring that if Byron was in regular contact with Mr. Walsh, surely he would be in touch with Walsh's daughter.

"No," she said. "Do you?"

"No."

"Surely you must have some leads," she said.

"We were looking for some from you," Margo said. "We have very little. We think he's quit Faslund to look

97

for a better position, and we base it partly on your father's having given permission for the personnel department to give out positive information about him to recruiters and head-hunters from other organizations."

Shirley had begun shaking her head as soon as Margo got to the part about his quitting Faslund for a better job. "I know Byron better than that," she said. "He's not that stupid. For one thing, he doesn't need or want a bigger challenge or salary or position. He couldn't have a better situation, if his goal was money and prestige and security. How could he have it any better? Besides, it's just not him. He a loyal company man."

"Then what's your guess?"

"I'm at a loss, and I'm serious," she said. "It's all I can do to keep my head above water. I paste on my smile every day and try to maintain some sense of normalcy, but it's driving me crazy. I plead with Father to give messages to Byron, but sometimes I wonder if Father himself really knows where he is."

"You don't really."

"No, I guess not. I guess I was just hoping. I hate it that Father knows and won't say anything. I need Byron, and I care about him. I miss him, and I'm worried about him. How can a father let his daughter go through that unnecessarily?"

"Unless he doesn't know how you feel about Byron."

"How can he not know?"

"Well, maybe he can," Margo said, "but apparently your father is under orders from Byron not to reveal his whereabouts."

"Yeah, I've heard that line too," she said, "but my father is never under orders from anyone unless he

98

wants to be. It's as if he enjoys keeping Byron from me."

"You think he's jealous of your relationship?"

"Oh, I'm sure. But this is more than that. This is serious business. This is going to do me in."

"Because you need Byron so much spiritually? He's discipling you?"

"No, he felt that that would better be handled by a woman from his church. She comes out every Friday morning, and we spend a couple of hours together. Alice Hertzler is her name. She's an angel."

Margo and I looked at each other. "Does her husband know about this?"

"Sure, but Byron has him sworn to secrecy."

"What do you think?" Margo asked her. "Any gut feelings about where he might be and why?"

She bit her lip. "I feel a little guilty about what I thought at first. I thought he had been fired. I thought he had displeased Father in some way—pushed him too far, annoyed him, whatever—because that is the only way Byron would ever be forced to leave Faslund."

"How? Did you think he might have pushed too hard in witnessing to him?"

"I just didn't know, but I did think it had to be something like that. I felt that way when I first heard about it, until Father came home from work that night. He was ashen, heartbroken, depressed. He drank more than he ever does before dinner. I was worried about him. But he told me it was true, that Byron was leaving the company in a month or so and that he honestly didn't feel he was going to be able to talk him out of it."

"And that convinced you that your father had no part in Byron's leaving?"

99

"Without a doubt. Father has never been one who is able to hide his emotions, a rare characteristic for a corporate president, I know. But I'm telling you, there were all night meetings, phone calls, everything you can think of to keep Byron at Faslund. Father hasn't put that much energy into one project since he acquired a Michigan paper mill a few years ago. But this was different because something personal was at stake."

"Didn't you talk to Byron at all during that last month?"

"A little, but he was very evasive. He said he would communicate with me later. I'm still counting on that. I tell Father everyday to remind Byron of that promise. For a while I was afraid I was the reason he was leaving the company. I thought maybe I had betrayed my feelings for him and scared him off."

"Your feelings for him? But you said—"

"I know what I said, and I'm sorry for misleading you. For lying to you actually. The reason I did that—which is only a reason and not an excuse—is because I didn't think my feelings for Byron were any of your business. That's what I should have told you, not what I did."

"How serious were your feelings for him?"

Miss Walsh stood and moved to the window where she stopped and turned around, her eyes focused on the floor. "It took a long time for me to sort them out," she began softly. "I had taken an interest in him early, then saw it wane. I was glad I hadn't expressed myself then, because it was clear he didn't share the attraction."

"He may have," Margo said. "But you're saying he didn't let on in any case."

"Right, OK. When we got into spiritual things, the old feeling for him returned, but again, I didn't express it and he didn't share it, or seem to share it anyway. It

100

was after I became a Christian that my true feelings for him hit me like a ton of bricks."

"You weren't just enamored with him because he had led you to Christ?"

"No, and I thought about that. But I was six months into my new faith before I realized I was in love with Byron. I've lived with it now for a year and a half, and I've never told anyone before."

"No one?"

"No one." And she sat down and cried.

Margo put a hand on her shoulder and asked, "Why did you never tell Byron? Couldn't you have at least written him a letter?"

She shook her head and fought for words that came in a raspy whisper. "I could tell he didn't feel the same about me. I didn't want to risk our friendship. It would have ended it for sure. Maybe it did anyway."

I said, "You think if he knew you loved him and didn't feel the same, it would be enough to make him throw away his job and his future?"

"I don't know," she sobbed. "He's a very principled man."

Margo stood and leaned over to put a hand on each of Miss Walsh's shoulders. "Shirley," she said, "do you honestly believe your father is the only person who knows where Byron is?"

She nodded miserably, dabbing at her eyes with a hankie. "I'm afraid so," she said. The phone rang and Shirley looked annoyed. "Ignore it," she said. "He'll remember I said no interruptions."

There was commotion above us, as if someone was running across the floor. "Who's up there?" Margo asked her.

"Mother," she said. "She's probably just hassling someone about something." The phone continued to ring until Shirley stood and lifted the receiver and replaced it, shaking her head.

More footsteps ran down the stairs at the end of the hall, and the phone rang again. Shirley was clearly angry now. She grabbed the receiver. "Albert, I told you, only emergen—what is it? Oh, no, no! Where's Mother?" She yanked the drape back and looked out the window. We saw her mother hustling into the backseat of an old Cadillac limousine. "Wait for me, Albert," Shirley added with authority, dropping the phone and running for the door.

The gardener was in the hall with her coat. She grabbed it and tugged it on as she bounded down the stairs and out the front door. She called over her shoulder, "It's Father!"

Chapter Twelve

Without our coats, we were hit full blast with the fall wind as we charged out the front door. "Bring up my car!" I hollered at the gardener.

I tried to keep an eye on the old limo as the gardener pulled up. "What's going on?" I asked him, almost pushing him aside as I slid in behind the wheel.

"I don't know, sir," he was saying slowly as we lurched away. "No one ever tells me—"

I hadn't realized how winding the long driveway was until I tried to take the curves at about forty miles per hour. I screeched up to the gate, looked both ways, and tore south on Green Bay Road in hot pursuit of the Walsh's backup limousine.

It was at times like this when I wished we had mobile radio units. I would have loved to have been able to let Wally know what was happening.

It didn't take long to overtake the Cadillac, and through its back window we could see Shirley embracing and comforting her mother. Albert, who was clearly not driving as fast as at least one of the women wished he would, noticed us in the rearview mirror and said something. The women glanced back. We waved, but Mrs. Walsh leaned forward and said something to Albert.

He spoke briefly on a radio transmitter and within a few minutes he had attracted two local police squad cars. The first settled in in front of him and with lights flashing and siren wailing led him through crowded, red-lighted intersections.

I tried to follow, but the second squad worked his way between the Cadillac and us and motioned me over. I stopped at the side of the road, but instead of pulling over himself, the officer rolled up beside me and said simply, "I can't let you follow the Walsh car. Understood?"

I nodded, and he drove away.

"Margo," I said, easing back into traffic, "do you think that means I could go to Faslund Paper, as long as I don't follow that car?"

"I certainly think so," she said.

I guessed that Mrs. Walsh was instructing Albert to take Green Bay Road, probably intending to get over to Sheridan Road and then Lake Shore Drive to the South Side. As quickly as I could, I went west to the Edens and shot south.

There was no way I'd beat Albert with his police escort, but with careful driving—and the rush hour traffic heading the other way—I reached the Faslund Paper corporate offices in less than thirty minutes.

The streets running in front and behind the building had been cordoned off. Several Chicago squad cars sat at odd angles, blue lights flashing. A paramedic ambulance sat off to one side, its lights off, attendants leaning back against its doors.

"Down here," Margo said, pointing to an alleyway not two blocks from the rear entrance of the building. That was where the activity seemed to be focused.

We ran to the edge of the roped off area and saw saw an eerie, gruesome sight. The white Mercedes Benz limousine Claude had used to transport Mr. Walsh downtown was parked directly in front of the walkway to the back door, and "Entrance Limited to Authorized Personnel," in the case of Faslund Paper, meant the brass.

The driver's side door was open, as were both back doors. From our vantage point, looking through the car from the driver's side, we could see Mr. Walsh stretched out on the back seat. His head lay near the middle of the seat, so his feet would have had to have been hanging out the other side, almost touching the ground.

"What do you make of it, Mar?" I asked.

"He's dead," she said flatly.

"How can you tell?"

"Because they're ignoring him. It's over. Whatever they did with him or for him didn't work. If he was ill, they'd be carting him off."

I stared into the backseat and could make out, even from thirty feet or so, that Walsh's tie had been removed and hung down to the floor. His overcoat, suit coat, vest, and shirt were unbuttoned and loosened from his chest.

"Heart attack?" I asked.

"Likely," Margo said. "As if it happened on the way and Claude raced here for help."

"But surely that car has a radio too. Why wouldn't he have called for help?"

Finally we spotted the black Cadillac with Mrs. Walsh now sitting on the passenger side in the front seat, her face in her hands. Albert stood outside the car, leaning back against the side of the hood, just in front of the driver's side door.

Shirley Walsh was talking animatedly and heatedly with two uniformed policemen and two men in business suits. One looked to be a plainclothes detective, though he wasn't dressed as obviously like a cop as Wally Festschrift had always been. The other wore an expensive suit and carried a thin, leather attaché, so I assumed he was with Faslund Paper.

As more people who appeared to be Faslund officials burst from a side entrance and hurried toward the scene, Margo tugged at my sleeve and pulled me closer to where Shirley Walsh was arguing with the men.

"If I can't see him," she was saying, "then please move him to where my mother and I *can* see him. This is a terrible ordeal for her, and look, here comes a bunch of people! I don't want them to see him stretched out there like that! Please!"

The man in the expensive suit, his thinning hair waving in the breeze, put an arm around Shirley and pulled her off to the side. "The ambulance is here now," he said, nodding toward an oversized station wagon with *Spellman-Lederer Funeral Home* on the door. "Shirley, there's something I must tell you. Whether you tell your mother is up to you."

I backed up to as close to Shirley and the man as I could without looking too conspicuous. I tried to appear as if I was just getting a better view of the action where Mr. Walsh was being removed from the limo. I could hear the man—whom Shirley referred to variously as Norm, Norman, and Godbey—very clearly.

"The timing on this is incredible, Shirl. Do you know his first meeting of the day today was with me?"

"So what, Norm? Of course I know that. I'm in touch with Mimi on his downtown schedule. Of course."

"Well, you couldn't have known, unless he himself told you, what the nature of our meeting was."

"Quit being so mysterious, Norman. What are you saying?"

106

"Shirley, your father was to sign a new will. He had me draw it up a couple of weeks ago, and he was going to sign it today. It would have been effective immediately."

"So what are you saying, Norm, that he had a premonition?"

"I don't know what I'm saying, honey, except that this is highly coincidental."

"So what was the nature of the new will? Did it include some new holdings or something?"

"No, it contained only one change, a major one. I'm not sure I should tell you."

"Get serious, Godbey, you're dying to tell me. What is it?"

"Well, originally he had left half his estate to your mother and the other half divided equally between his surviving children."

"Yes?"

"When your brother died, he asked me about changing the will and I said it wouldn't be necessary because the language, referring to the surviving offspring, covered the death. The proceeds from the estate would be divided up two ways instead of three."

"Yes, yes."

"About six years ago he had me rewrite the will and include Huttmann — you know, Byron, the guy who used to work here — as a recipient in equal share to that of the surviving children. I'm sorry if that upsets you, but that's what he did. I didn't know he was that close to Huttmann, but I heard the rumors, you know."

"Mr. Godbey, I'm watching my dead father being loaded into a car. Now will you get on with it?"

"Well, I don't know how to explain it, Shirley, but this new will would have changed all the language back to the original."

"Meaning?"

"Meaning he was totally cutting Huttmann back out of the estate. There would be no mention of his name, as if it had never been in there in the first place."

"You're right, Norman. You shouldn't have told me in the first place. His will, except as how it relates to me, is none of my business. I'd rather not have known."

"I'm sorry, Shirley. But what do you think of it?"

"I don't know, Norm, and right now I don't care."

She turned and walked back toward her mother, still waiting in the car. I intercepted her. "Miss Walsh," I said. "I'm very sorry. What happened?"

She turned and stopped, then broke down as Margo and I embraced her and walked her back to her mother. Albert opened the back door for us but remained outside the car.

"Mother, these are the Spences. They're sort of friends of Byron's and have been looking for him."

I thought it significant that she had called us "sort of" friends of a man we'd never met. Mrs. Walsh turned her head only partially toward us and nodded slightly. Her jaw was set, her face grim. There were no tears, and her bright, flowery outfit was juxtaposed against the scene of her husband's death.

Shirley spoke in a barely audible whisper. "Claude thought father was napping on the way in, though that's not common unless he's had an unusually late and busy night—which is also uncommon. Claude realized something was wrong when Father leaned forward involuntarily while the car was stopping."

"When he arrived?"

"I don't think so. A mile or so from here. He felt it would be better to get him to the office before trying to call for help. The medics think Father was dead when

108

he arrived here. There was no pulse, no vital signs. They tried CPR."

"They must have been here a long time," Margo said. "It's been quite a while since he left home."

Mrs. Walsh had buried her face in her hands again, and now, muffled by her fingers, came a request. "Shirley, can't we see him or go somewhere or do something rather than just sit here?"

Shirley gently touched her mother's shoulder. "It won't be long," she said.

A detective approached the car, showing his badge to Mrs. Walsh through the front window. She looked up and shook her head, pointing to Shirley in the back. "My daughter," she said.

"You're the daughter?" the detective said to Margo. She motioned to Shirley.

"Something I need you to identify," he said. "Can you come with me?"

I stepped out to let her out, and she said, "Come, please."

The detective eyed me, and Shirley told him simply, "He's with me."

"Whatever," the cop said.

He led us to the funeral home ambulance where his partner was crouched near the back, bagging a revolver. It was a Smith and Wesson thirty-eight caliber with a six-inch barrel, most commonly used as a police target pistol.

"Do you recognize it?" the detective said, holding the clear plastic bag up in front of her face.

"Should I?"

"It was found in the pocket of your father's suit coat. Not the overcoat. The suit coat."

"It looks brand new," I said.

"It *is* brand new," the detective said. "Not more'n a

109

couple of months old. New model. Didn't make 'em last year. You recognize it or not, Mrs. ah—?"

"Miss," she said. "Walsh. And no, I don't. He never owned a gun. Never hunted, never practiced, never collected them. Wouldn't know what to do with one is my guess."

"He knew how to load it. The chamber was full, and he had the rest of the box in his other pocket."

Shirley just stood shaking her head. A uniformed patrol officer jogged up. "Sergeant," he said, addressing the plainclothesman, and he whispered new information. As he moved away, the detective turned to us again.

"The driver, this, uh, Claude Heckman, says your father had him stop at a sporting goods store just inside the city limits. Had to get off the expressway and everything."

"What did he have Claude buy for him?"

"That's just it. He insisted on going in by himself. Heckman says he came out about twenty minutes later, empty handed."

"So?"

"So he apparently bought the gun on the way to work. He bought it to use it, Miss Walsh. The strain of it all aggravated his heart condition and killed him. Know anyone he might have wanted to settle a score with today?"

Shirley couldn't answer. "He didn't have a heart condition," she managed.

"I don't mean to be cold, ma'am," the detective said. "But he's got one now."

Chapter Thirteen

It was at that moment that I was reminded that we had left our coats at the Walsh estate and how brisk the day really was. Yes, the detective's comment *had* been cold, but he had a point.

I wanted to ask Shirley about her conversation with the corporate counsel, Norman Godbey. But she hadn't been aware that I had overheard it, and if she thought about it, she'd realize that it could—in a way—make it appear that Byron Huttmann had been her father's intended victim.

Apparently she had thought about it because she volunteered nothing to the detective, even when Godbey approached.

"If you are through with Miss Walsh," he said, "I'd like to update her on arrangements."

The detective merely left his card and told her he would be in touch with her.

Godbey put his arm around her shoulder and led her back to the Cadillac where her mother sat alone, weeping. I saw Margo heading for our car. "I'll handle things for now," Godbey was telling Shirley. "You go home, and I'll call you when you can bring your mother and finalize the arrangements. Would you like me to call your sister too?"

"No, I will. And thanks, Norman."

"I'll see you back at your place," I said.

She looked distracted and confused. "We won't stay," I said. "We just need to get our coats."

"Oh, it's all right," she said. "I think I'd like you to stay, if I can't find Byron."

I opened the back door for her. "I overheard you talking with Godbey earlier," I said.

She flinched and shot me a doubletake. "They didn't have a falling out," she said quickly. "I would have known. It would have shown. And it didn't."

"I believe you," I said. "But it doesn't look good just now, does it?"

She didn't respond.

On the way north Margo told me that Mrs. Walsh had kicked her out of the car.

"Really?" I said. "What had you said?"

"I just tried to console her at first, then I asked her if she wanted me to pray for her. She hit the ceiling. She said she certainly didn't want anyone praying for her when she didn't even know who they were. She said, 'Who are you anyway and what are you doing here? Why don't you just get lost?'"

"She actually told you to get lost?"

Margo nodded. "I don't think she'll be too excited to see me again at her home."

She was probably right. But when we arrived, Mrs. Walsh was distracted, as we all were, by someone waiting on her front steps. Trench coat crumpled beneath him, elbows on knees, white socks and bare shin showing beneath his polyester suit pants, it was Wally Festschrift in all his bulk.

He looked as if he thought he belonged there, but he wasn't smiling, and he stood when the Cadillac's doors opened. After awkward introductions and glares from the older Walsh woman, Shirley and Margo and Wally and I met in Shirley's office while Mrs. Walsh and the help disappeared.

"I really should be with Mother," Shirley said several times, but each time we agreed she said her mother really wanted to be alone. The phone began ringing almost incessantly, and Shirley instructed Albert what to tell the callers.

"I know this is a difficult time for you, Miss Walsh," Wally said, "but when I heard about your father's death on the news and realized how close he was to Byron Huttmann, I thought I should at least come and find out what my people had discovered. If you're not up to talking, I'll understand."

She said nothing. I asked if it would be all right if I told Wally what she had told us earlier. She looked stony and asked to see me in private. We stepped into the hall and heard phones ringing all over the house.

"Mr. Spence," she said, "the only reason I felt free to tell you such personal information about myself and Byron was because you and your wife seemed to understand what had happened to me. Do you realize that not even Byron knows how I feel about him?"

"Yes, but—"

"Do you realize that within a few minutes my relatives will start arriving and that this will keep up for the weekend and through whenever the funeral is?"

"Well, we certainly don't—"

"Do you realize that my father's death hasn't even sunk in yet? I don't know how it will affect me when it does. I feel as if I'm about to go crazy, as if God hasn't answered the most important prayer of my life, as if I'm alone in the world."

"We care about you," I said.

"I just met you!" she said, almost shouting and breaking into tears.

"If you don't want me to tell Mr. Festschrift anything, I certainly won't."

She nodded as if that's what she wanted.

"And if you want us to just leave you alone for a week or two, we can do that too."

She shrugged, her face in her hands.

"But let me tell you this: Margo and I already feel a kinship to you. That may not mean much to you right now, but it will soon, and we want you to know we're available if you need us."

She stared at the floor, as if hoping I would finish and be gone. "Can I tell you one more thing?" I asked.

She sighed and looked up at me wearily. She blinked slowly, waiting.

"I just want to tell you that if there's anyone on the face of the earth who can turn up Byron Huttmann, it's Wally Festschrift. He was the best homicide detective in Chicago not many years ago, and—"

She held up both hands. "I don't care who he was or is. I appreciate your offer, but I need to go somewhere and scream. Understand?"

"Sure, I'm sorry. Forgive us for—"

"What is it, Albert?" she said, noticing the butler at the top of the stairs.

"Just wondered if you wanted any messages, ma'am," he said. "Several have called."

"Relatives?"

"And friends."

"You told them we'd get back to them with specifics?"

"Yes, ma'am."

"And you have their numbers?"

"Yes, all but one, ma'am."

"Which one?"

"Mr. Huttmann."

She paled. "Byron called?"

Albert nodded. "He asked that I express his deepest sympathy."

"But he didn't leave a number, an address, anything?"

"No, ma'am."

"He said nothing else?"

"Uh, not really, no."

"What do you mean, 'not really'?"

"Well, he asked me a rather strange question, Miss Walsh."

She looked at me and then back at Albert. She approached him, and he whispered in her ear.

"And what did you tell him, Albert?" she said, on the verge of tears again.

"Why, I told him no, ma'am. I told him I thought certainly not."

She turned and walked past me and into her office. Albert stood staring after her, then went slowly back down the stairs. I followed her in. "Mr. Festschrift," she said.

Wally struggled to his feet, startled. "I want you to find Byron Huttmann for me. Not for Lyssa Jack or the police or Mr. Godbey or anyone else. I will pay double your normal fee, but you must report back only to me, no one else. Understood?"

"No, ma'am," Wally said. "Can't do it. I have a client. I will look earnestly for Mr. Huttmann for her, and I will be happy to report our findings to anyone who wants to know. Would you like to be on that list?"

"I have a lot of personal, specific information that may help you," she said. "Mr. or Mrs. Spence have my permission to tell you."

"That will be helpful," Wally said, "but I must insist that you allow me to do it on my terms, not yours. I won't take your money, and I won't ace Lyssa Jack out of the picture."

Shirley flopped down in a chair and looked up at Margo and me. "You agree with him?" she asked.

"Always," I said.

"We've learned to," Margo added.

"All right," she said. "You can tell Mr. Festschrift whatever you want. Just let me know what you find."

"What made you change your mind, Shirley?" I asked. "What did Byron ask Albert when he called?"

"He asked if Father's death had been a suicide, which, of course, it was not."

Back at our office, Wally put Margo and me on the phones, her to try one more time to locate the Huttmann family in Traverse City, Michigan, and me to check with the phone company about the calls that had been received at the Walsh estate within the last two hours.

It didn't take long to determine that while there had been a lot of telephone activity, only one of the calls had lasted long enough to be computer-recorded by the phone company. That was one from southern Wisconsin, but a quick check found that it was a cousin of the Walshes.

Margo found that the family was still apparently not home, so Wally had her check with the local police department in Traverse City. They confirmed that the family had asked for spot checks of their residence while they spent two weeks in northern Illinois.

"That narrows it down," Wally groused. "If they're visiting Byron, they're within a hundred and twenty miles of his old apartment, right?"

We nodded. The phone rang. "Just a second," Wally said when the caller had identified himself. He put the call on hold and told us it was an old buddy of his from the Chicago Police Department. When he punched the call back in, he had it on the amplifier box so we could hear it.

"C'mon, Wally," the voice was saying, "I've only got a minute. I thought you'd wanna know. That Walsh death could have been a suicide."

"What makes you think so?"

"Well, he died from a heart attack, but he wanted to die. They found a note in his briefcase. Listen to this: 'The pain of losing two sons is too great. Forgive me.' It was dated yesterday."

"I don't get it," Wally said. "What two sons did he lose?"

"We don't know," came the voice. "His only son was killed in a car crash several years ago. Maybe he had an illegitimate son or something, or maybe they lost a baby in childbirth or before. Who knows? We're checking. You want me to let you know?"

"Yeah. And thanks," Wally said, hanging up. "So, he was gonna snuff himself with that revolver. Pretty expensive way to go. More'n two hundred bucks."

"But he died coincidentally?" Margo said. "Sounds a bit farfetched, doesn't it?"

"I guess," Wally said. "Unless they find poison in his system. Wouldn't be the first time somebody poisoned himself and then didn't like either the side effects, the slowness, or the thought of its failing. Used a gun just in case. I remember a guy once who killed himself with a shotgun blast in the mouth, and we found enough

117

phenobarbitol in his system to kill a horse. Got impatient, I guess."

Lyssa Jack phoned, and the amplifier was still engaged. Wally told her all we knew so far.

"Does that mean Byron's dead?" she asked haltingly.

"I don't know," Wally said. "I have no way of knowing. If his family is visiting him, he can't be too hard to find. It's just that we're stymied. We have no idea where to start looking for him."

From the sounds on the other end of the line it was clear that Lyssa wanted to chew us out, to swear at us, to ride us, to push us. But she said little. "You can help if you know anything else, honey," Wally said. "Anything at all. Hang on a second," he added, punching up another ringing line. "Hello, EH Agency. No, that was Spence. Just a minute."

He handed me the phone. "Sir," a woman's voice said. "Illinois Bell calling. Just wanted to make you aware that calls to the number you were requesting recently are being recorded at that residence. I hadn't noticed it on the card when you called before, but apparently the call recorder was installed a couple of years ago. You'd need authorization from the customer to see the log, of course."

Bingo.

Chapter Fourteen

When Wally Festschrift swings into action, there's nobody anywhere who can compete. He sweet-talked Shirley Walsh into not only investigating the whereabouts of the printouts of the phone conversations to the estate, but also into having them copied for him.

Into the middle of the night we worked at eliminating the names of relatives and known friends whose numbers matched those on the printout. The six numbers no one recognized would be called the first thing Friday morning.

When they had been narrowed down and divvied up between us, there was suddenly nothing left to do.

"Do you realize," Wally said, rolling a chair into the middle of the floor, leaning back, and sprawling in it, "that one of these numbers is where Byron Huttmann called from today? For the first time in this crazy case, we're warm. We're on his heels. We can smell him."

"Can you?" Margo said, stretching and yawning. "I have this fear we're going to find out that one of these numbers is a pay phone in the middle of nowhere."

Wally erupted into a bellow. "Yeah!" he said. "Just our luck, huh? Well, there's nothin' we can do about it at this time of the morning. What say we meet back here in seven hours and find this guy? Besides the two numbers each of you has, Margo, you let Lyssa Jack know what we're up to — we owe her that, at least — and Philip, you try the family in Traverse City one more time.

The phone rang. Wally flipped the box on and picked up the receiver. "Anybody callin' this late knows who they got," he announced into the receiver. "Your dime."

"Mr. Festschrift?" came Shirley Walsh's pleasant but troubled voice.

"One and the same," Wally said. "We're knockin' off for the evening, and we have nothing yet, if that's what you're wondering."

"I wasn't wondering anything really, Mr. Festschrift. I, uh, just thought you should know something. My mother remembered that Father wanted to be cremated, and she checked with Mr. Godbey. Sure enough, it's in his will, and it calls for cremation within forty-eight hours of the death. I didn't know if that made any difference to you or not."

"Hm," Wally growled, furrowing his brow. "I don't know. I guess not, but I should think homicide would be worried about it if there's any physical evidence they need and might have missed. Was there an autopsy?"

"Yes, but there's been no report of foreign substances yet. I don't know how long that takes."

"Not long, but if he's cremated before they discover poison, they might want to check more closely for signs of forced consumption. Hypodermic needle holes, contusions around the mouth, that kind of a thing. Problem is, as far as I know, there's no reason to suspect a homicide at this point is there? I mean other than the fact that it seemed from his carrying a weapon that he may have had an enemy."

120

"He had a lot of enemies, sir. People in his position always do."

"I know, but I mean a current one, a hot one. Philip told me about the will change, Miss Walsh. That could implicate Byron, you know."

"Why did he feel the need to tell you that?"

"You said he could tell me anything he wanted that would help me find Byron."

There was silence on the other end, and I was dying, wishing Wally hadn't told her.

"What does Mr. Spence think of that?" she asked finally, timidly.

"He doesn't think anything more than I do about it," Wally said. "It's a puzzle, that's all. A clue. We can't make it make sense. You say they didn't have a falling out, so how would you assess it? You have to admit it appears that your father cut him out of the will when he couldn't talk Byron into staying with the company."

"I'd rather not think about it."

"Well, neither would I, Miss Walsh. Neither would I. But it seems you'd be as interested to know precisely how your father died as you are in finding Mr. Hutt-mann."

"Not if Byron is implicated I'm not. Until someone proves otherwise, I'm satisfied that Father died of a heart attack."

"And the purchase of the revolver?"

"What about it?" she said.

"That's *my* question."

"I have no idea. I can't figure that one at all. Totally out of character."

"Almost as if he wasn't himself today?"

"Right," she said.

"As if he were acting on impulse or out of passion,

the same way he had when he wrote his surrogate son out of his will?"

Shirley didn't respond, sensing where Wally was going.

"Almost as if he was temporarily not really with it?"

"You've got his defense all figured out, Mr. Festschrift," Shirley said with ice in her voice. "But you forget he committed no crime. He bought a gun he never used, even if he wanted to or planned to. He doesn't need a temporary insanity plea, even if it was a suicide, which nothing has indicated yet either."

"You're forgetting his note."

"How do you know about the note?"

"I know everything," Wally said. "Don't underestimate me."

"Excuse me," she said with sarcasm. "But all the note tells me is that he may have purchased the gun with suicide in mind. But he never got to it. He didn't have to. The strain of it all, whatever was bothering him and made him buy it in the first place, got to him before his irrationality did."

"What would you say if I told you that Byron Huttmann was found dead?"

Margo and I stared at Wally, shaking our heads violently. Shirley said nothing.

"That he was found murdered," Wally continued.

Margo rolled her eyes and walked away from Wally.

"Just so you won't have your own heart attack, Miss Walsh, it isn't true," he said. "I just wondered how you'd react. It could happen, you know. We could find him that way. And then all your pet theories and pat answers go right out the window."

"You're a cold one, aren't you?" she asked. "You can say those things to me on the night of my father's death?"

"Hey, lady, I want it to turn out the same way you do, you know? I just have to get you out of La-La Land. Your father has a fairly normal conversation with my people, a little tension maybe — nothing serious, and on his way into work he buys a gun and dies before he gets a chance to use it. Now who was he gonna use it on? Himself? Huttmann? I don't know. Do you know?"

"The note was dated yesterday."

"Well," Wally said, hesitating, "that *is* significant. That makes the suicide premeditated, if it was indeed suicide."

"Well, he never got it done," she said. "His heart gave out first."

"I'll leave that conclusion to the coroner. Meanwhile, I'm looking for your Byron Huttmann and hoping he wasn't the target of your father's wrath or the direct cause of his death. I do find it interesting that you'd sooner label your father a potential suicide than to think he could use that gun on someone else."

"He couldn't, but don't think it's not painful to think he could have killed himself. He must have been terribly hurt and distressed. I thought I knew him better."

"But what you really hate to think about is the fact that he might have wanted to use that gun on Huttmann."

"He didn't."

"You keep telling yourself that."

"I will. Because for some reason, even Byron had an inkling it might have been a suicide. If he had seen Father recently, which I know he did, he would have known something was troubling him."

"Or he might have simply wanted to plant the suicide idea in your mind," Wally said. "Just like he might have planted the suicide note in your father's brief-case."

"You're reaching now, Mr. Festschrift. You have a quick mind, but you're stretching its capacity. That note was written in my father's own hand."

"With his own pen on his own paper perhaps, but you might want a graphoanalyst to be sure it wasn't forged. Who would know your father's handwriting better than Byron?"

"I would. And Mother would. And his secretary would."

"So we have four suspects."

"Good night, Mr. Festschrift," she said, hanging up without waiting for his response.

Margo returned and slumped onto the desk next to Wally. "What *was* that all about, Wally?" she demanded. "That wasn't like you at all! I mean, I've seen you ride *suspects* and make them defend or implicate themselves, but what a merciless way to treat someone who's just lost a loved one."

"Yeah," Wally said, standing and reddening as I had never seen him do in front of Margo, "maybe you know a better approach with all your years in the business."

"Wally!" Margo said, stunned. "I'm sorry. You know I would never dream of trying to tell you how to do your work. I just don't understand. You're not yourself. You're defensive. What is it?"

Wally charged toward the door. "Well, maybe veteran detectives deserve the right to an off night once in a while too. You ever think of that?"

And he was gone, down the hall to his apartment. We heard the door slam, and Margo covered her mouth and cried.

"What's with him?" I said, embracing her. She just

124

shrugged and shook her head. "I'm going to find out," I said.

"Don't," she said. "Let him be. Something's obviously bothering him."

I really wanted to talk with him, but she was right. We tidied up the place, turned off the lights, locked the door, and headed for the stairs. We heard Wally's door open.

"Hey," he grunted. "C'mere a minute."

Chapter Fifteen

When we arrived at Wally's door he swung it open wide and gave Margo a big bear hug.

She sobbed on his shoulder. "I'm sorry, Wally," she said. "You know I'd never say or do anything to hurt you."

"Hey, hey," he said, stroking her hair with his fleshy hand. "My fault. My fault. We gotta talk. Something happened to me today."

He directed us to a dark green, hard fabric, foam rubber filled couch that tended to sink with you as you sat down. We stared at the big man through our knees as he sat in a musty old easy chair. He kicked his shoes off and loosened his tie.

"Don't give up on me, Mar," he said. "You never would, would ya?"

She shook her head and grinned tight-lipped at him.

His chest was still heaving from the effort of bustling from the office and then calling us back. He sat catching his breath for a moment, then sighed deeply and told us his story.

"I heard about Walsh dying, and I thought maybe I could catch you guys out there. I called a couple of times and got no answer, but I didn't know what that meant. I hurried out and down the stairs, and at first I forgot I had parked across the street because of that expansion bash Allyson and her mother were throwing today in the boutique. Did you remember that?"

I shook my head. Margo nodded. "I wish I could have gone," she said. But Wally wasn't listening.

"Anyway, they had asked if they could have the extra parking places, and I'm easy, so I'm parked at the drugstore across the street, and by the time I remember that, I've been around the building trying to recall where I parked. So I'm upset, in a hurry, mad at myself, and feeling foolish when I finally remember my car is in plain sight."

He shifted his weight, and I could see the strain on his face. He was becoming emotional, but if I hadn't known better I would have thought this was one of his long, drawn out, hilarious, self-effacing jokes. But it wasn't.

"I start jogging across the street, as only I can, and this kid comes around the corner off Glencoe Road in a Trans Am. He's movin', almost on two wheels, OK? And he's gonna hit me; that's all there is to it. I can tell from looking at him that he hasn't even seen me yet, and I freeze. Me freezing, can you beat that? So I take one more big step and dive headfirst like I'm stealing second base, only I've still got my head turned toward the kid and I'm praying he'll see me, 'cause if he keeps coming without seeing me and he does nothing like swerve or brake or back off or something, nothing's gonna save me, OK?"

Wally's voice was shaky, and neither Margo nor I could move. It was as if we were there, reliving it with him.

"You think I'm using that line about praying as a figure of speech, but I'm not. They talk about your life flashing before you? I don't know about that, but I never felt closer to God than I did right then. And I'm thinkin', if I get snuffed, I won't be close to God. I'll have missed my chance. You won't believe it, but while

I'm sliding across the street on my gut and chewing up my hands" — he showed us both skinned palms — "and tearing up my knees, I'm thinking about God and how shocked I was to hear that Walsh had died so suddenly and how I might be doing just the same."

His face was red and he was sweating. I had never seen him quite like this. He shifted around again and tried to sit with one leg tucked up under him — which he would be able to stand for fewer than ninety seconds because of the obstruction his weight would be to the circulation in his leg.

"It's like everything is in slow motion," he said, "and at the last instant I see the kid's eyes hit me, and I think he takes his foot off the gas, that's all. I hear a backfire, so I figure that's it. My right hand crunches up against the front tire of my own parked car and my body follows, sort of jamming me up against the fender, and I realize I've hit the side of the front bumper with my head."

He stood and bent over, and we could see a long scab beneath the thinning hair line.

"The kid keeps going, of course, but I think he looks back to make sure he hasn't hit me. I'm so shaky and wobbly that I just sit there for a minute, and I don't mind telling you I honestly don't know if he's run over me or not. I start checking everything out. Fingers, hands, toes, ankles, feet, knees. Everything's working, but I can hardly stand up. Pain in the chest much? Ooh, I was scared. I get in the car, but I don't drive off right away."

Wally had slowed down. The story had become difficult for him to tell. He was now sitting on the front edge of the chair, earnestly looking into our eyes, elbows on his knees.

"Well, I, uh, I broke down and cried."

"Oh, Wally," Margo said, reaching for his hand.

"I, uh, thought about how easy it was for somebody to die. I mean, I've been around death and dead bodies all my life. I've seen people die. I even killed a man once. In the line of duty, of course. And I never met this Walsh. He shouldn't have meant a thing to me. He was just a person in a case. If you hadn't been seeing him today, it wouldn't have even made that big an impression on me that he all of a sudden dies. But for some reason, it got to me. And then I almost buy it in the street in front of my own office and apartment."

"What did you pray about, Wally?" Margo asked gently.

"It was crazy," he said. "I asked God how come He thought I wasn't mad at the kid. I usually swear at drivers like that, especially kids, or give 'em an obscene gesture. Or both. You've seen me do it. Sometimes I even chase 'em down and scare 'em a little. He deserved it. They all do. But I wasn't mad at this kid. It was as if he was put there for a purpose. I was supposed to forget my car and trot across that street right then as he whipped around the corner. Somehow I knew that. How could I be mad at him for that when it was meant to be?"

Neither of us wanted to comment on his elementary theology, knowing that it could very well have been true that God chose that way to deal with Wally Festschrift.

"Did you feel God answered you, Wally?" Margo said.

"How could I know?" he asked.

"Sometimes you just sense it," I said. "God can speak to us through our minds and consciences."

"Uh-huh," he said, suddenly even more serious, as if something had just come clear to him. "I did feel like there was something I was supposed to do, but I couldn't put my finger on it."

"Something you felt God wanted you to do?" I said. He nodded.

"Did He want you to make your transaction with Him, to buy into your security so you won't have to worry about dying suddenly?"

He shrugged. "I don't know. I guess so. I felt like I had made contact with God for the first time. I knew I wasn't mad at that kid, and it was almost like I knew God had put him there and me there for a reason, but as soon as I felt a little better and caught my breath, I just headed out to the Walsh place and I've been irritable ever since."

It was almost as if Wally was waiting for one of us to pray with him or say something that would close the conversation. But for some reason, neither of us felt led to do it. He had been so clear for so long that he wanted to do this on his own. He didn't want to be led, pushed, cajoled, badgered, anything.

So we both sat in silence, looking at each other and at him and smiling awkwardly. "I suppose I know what I've got to do," he said. "But I just wanted you to know I felt bad about the way I was tonight. And I'll have to apologize to Miss Walsh too, won't I? See how I was on a death kick, asking that poor woman about her dead father and insinuating that Huttmann had been found dead?" Wally swore, almost inaudibly. "Excuse me," he said, smiling sheepishly.

That night we prayed for Wally as never before. In the morning he was bright and cheerful and energetic.

Margo tried to hint around to see what he might have done after we had left, but he kept avoiding personal conversation — almost as if he hadn't heard her, though once he said, "No time to talk! Get on the phones!"

Margo brought Lyssa Jack up to date, and she insisted on coming in to the office, certain we would track Byron down that day. I finally reached the Huttmann family in Traverse City, Michigan, and learned that they had been visiting Byron the last couple of days, detouring on the way home from their vacation.

It was hardly surprising that Mrs. Huttmann put Mr. Huttmann on the phone, and there was no way he would tell a stranger — claiming to be a private detective or not — where his son was. He said he would be happy to pass a message along and that maybe Byron would call me if he wanted.

"No," I said. "I think he's already been made aware that we're looking for him. Do you know Lyssa Jack, sir?"

"No, but Byron did mention that name this week for the first time. Apparently he had been very fond of the girl, but it just didn't work out. He's eager that she not know of his whereabouts either."

"But he's all right? I mean we shouldn't worry about his safety or anything?"

"It would be correct to say that you should not worry about his safety, yes."

I tried a few more ploys to garner any information at all but came up empty handed. "Why didn't you tell him you were a Christian?" Wally asked. "Try anything."

"Why didn't *you*?" I said, but he wouldn't bite.

When we had finished our calling, we huddled in

131

Wally's office. "At this point," he said, "we can do one of two things. We can tell Lyssa Jack that we are satisfied that the target of our investigation does not want to be found. That he has not been abducted, is not in danger, and does not want to see her. She'll be here soon and I would normally be most comfortable telling her that."

"But doesn't it drive you nuts, Wally?" I said. "Wondering where he is?"

"That's not the question," Margo said, as we heard Bonnie letting Lyssa in the front door. "The question is, What is the other of the two options you said we had? Something tells me that the second is one that will keep us on the trail."

Wally was beaming, eyes twinkling. "She's a natural, Philip," he said. "You're a hard worker and a plodder. A good one. But this one," he said, patting her shoulder, "she was born with it."

"All right," I said, only a little jealous of my wife, begrudgingly aware that he was drop-dead right, "what are we up to now?"

"Well," he said, taking a deep breath, "my calls were both dead ends. One was a wrong number, and the other was a catering service calling about some shindig Walsh was going to have in a couple of weeks.

"So, while you were making your calls and striking out too, Philip, I checked in with both the Chicago and the local police departments. Chicago is looking for Huttmann."

Our mouths dropped open. "You *are* kidding," Margo said.

Wally sat there grinning.

"Why?"

"Because of something the lawyer told them about the will."

132

"The cremation?"

"No, the cutting of Huttmann from any inheritance."

"But that won't hold up because Walsh never signed it."

"Still, it's a possible motive for murder, and they want to check it out. I'd like to find Huttmann first for several reasons. For one, we'd get paid more. And for another, from everything we've learned about him, he's no killer. In fact, how could he know he'd been written out of the will?"

"Unless Godbey told him."

"Unlikely that Godbey knows where he is."

"Or Mrs. Walsh."

"She may have been the one who told Godbey to tell the police, but she wouldn't have known about the new will until she checked with Godbey about the cremation."

Wally had been right. I had struck out the same as he had. The numbers I checked turned out to be a telephone solicitation service and an old friend of Mr. Walsh who had heard of his death.

Margo had been the only successful one of the bunch. She turned up a pay phone in southern Wisconsin that we would need to check out with Shirley, hoping she would know of someone who might call from there.

The other number she identified was of the Long Acre Convalescent and Rehabilitation Institute just south of Zion, Illinois. We assumed it was a retiree from the company or some other elderly crony of Walsh's, but at least we had a couple of numbers to check out.

It wasn't much, but it was all we had. And we agreed with Wally. If anyone else felt Huttmann was worth finding, we did too. And first.

133

Chapter Sixteen

Wally seemed depressed and disappointed when Shirley Walsh said she remembered the call from the pay phone. "It was one of my uncles from Monroe, Wisconsin," she said. "He had heard about Father on the radio as he was driving home and said he stopped as soon as he could to call us."

Wally asked her about the Long Acre Convalescent and Rehabilitation Institute near Zion. "Yes, I'm familiar with LACRI because Father supports it. They probably were calling about a benefit or something, though I'm surprised they didn't call him at the office. That's all handled through his secretary downtown and his lawyer. I would hope that Mr. Godbey wouldn't have given out our home number."

Wally asked Margo to check with the phone company and find out if the LACRI phone used to call the Walsh home was a central or office number as opposed to a pay phone or private room phone. "Also check back with Shirley and see if anyone at the house remembers a business call from LACRI."

When Wally and I emerged from his office, hands thrust deep in our pockets, our dejection must have been apparent to Lyssa. "No leads?" she asked. "I thought you had it narrowed down."

"We're gonna check out a place," Wally said, "but

we're not optimistic. Margo's makin' a couple more calls first."

"I want to go with you," Lyssa said.

"Nah, you don't," Wally said, brushing her off. "It's a hundred to one shot. Anyway—"

"I'm going with you," she said.

"No. Anyway, even if we found Byron there, we have clear indication that he doesn't want to see you."

"I'm going with you, Mr. Festschrift," Lyssa said coldly. "I'm paying the bills, and I don't see how Byron has a choice about seeing me. I could get him for breach of promise, you know."

Wally looked shocked. "Breach of promise? Not from anything you've told us so far about what went on between you two. Anyway, I thought you wanted to find your long lost love, not someone to sue."

"I don't want to sue him, of course," she said. "But obviously you've talked to him and know where he is and—"

"No, we don't!"

"Then who'd you talk to who told you he doesn't want to see me?"

"I'm not sure I want to tell you that."

"You forget, Mr. Festschrift, why you were talking to his family in the first place. I hired you, remember? I'm paying for that phone call. Was he with his family on vacation?"

"No, but they saw him on the way back."

"Here? In the Chicago area?"

"We don't know."

"I'm going with you when you find out."

"You might follow us, but you'll not be riding along."

Lyssa was burning when Margo came out of Wally's office. Margo sized up the situation and gave Wally his answers in code. "Pay phone in the lobby," she said. "And no, no one remembers."

"Let's go," Wally said, yanking his coat off the hook. We followed him out and down the stairs toward his car with Lyssa jogging along behind us and whining, "Your car will hold four. C'mon, sir, let me ride along. C'mon, please? At least slow down so I can follow you!"

Wally did that.

"You don't mind if she follows?" Margo asked as he waited at the corner before pulling out onto Glencoe Road so Lyssa had time to get out of the parking lot.

"Nah. I probably should have let her ride along. She's right. We're doing this for her. But I can't alienate Huttmann by making it too obvious that we brought her along."

"You really think we're going to find him at this, uh—"

"LACRI," Wally said.

"Yeah," I said, "at this LACRI place?"

"Not really. It's a long shot, but right now it's all we've got."

"Then what difference does it make if she follows or rides with us?" Margo asked.

"It's just that I have something to tell you two that I don't need anyone else to hear yet."

"You think we're going to find Huttmann at this place after all?" I said.

"No," he said. "It's not about that. It's about something I did last night after you left."

And he told us about how he had prayed and told God that he knew he needed Him. "I remembered all that stuff you've been telling me. We've talked about it enough times. The biggest thing I had to get over was the feeling that I wasn't ready, I wasn't good enough. I

136

always wanted a little more time to get myself in better shape, to cut out a few things, to add a few things. But you know, even though thinking about God and Christ and all of that the last year or so has changed me in little ways, nothing I ever did or tried to do or not do ever really made a difference in me. I couldn't make myself better. Oh, I was surprised at myself now and then and realized that I was thinking about different things than I ever had before, but as hard as I tried to get myself into a position where I thought God might accept me, I could never make it. And I realized that even if I changed almost completely, I still wouldn't qualify."

"Neither would we," Margo said quietly.

"Well, I know," Wally said. "And the first time you and Philip told me that I thought you were being falsely modest and all that. That really threw me. But I understand it now. It became clear to me with some of those verses you showed me. Nobody qualifies and the sooner they recognize that, the sooner they'll accept God rather than waiting for Him to accept them."

"This is an important step in your life," Margo said.

"Oh, I know that. I—"

"No, I mean this step right here. What you did last night, yes, that's the most important, but almost as important is telling us about it. It'll help solidify it for you if you can tell us exactly what happened to you when you prayed. Do you know?"

Wally stole a glance at her before looking back to his driving. "Yeah," he said solemnly, "I know. God saved me. He forgave me because of what Christ did for me. And I believe. I believe it all, the whole package. And I'm happy."

"You're a believer," I said.

"Yeah. I'm a believer. Just like you and Earl."

"And lots of people you're going to meet from now on."

"That'll be nice," Wally said. And his belief was written all over his face.

At the Long Acre Convalescent and Rehabilitation Institute, a sprawling, single story facility that covered several acres, Wally pleaded with Lyssa Jack to wait for us in her car. He promised to let her know if we turned up anything and that he wouldn't keep her from seeing Byron if he could help it.

The receptionist had never heard of anyone named Byron Huttmann and assured Wally that there was no one registered under that name. "Is this an elderly relative?" she asked.

"Well, no, no ma'am, not elderly, no."

"Well, we have so few patients who aren't elderly. Not more than a dozen. And they're all in this facility because they generally don't like being integrated into the elderly population."

Wally gave Margo and me the eye. He has a way of doing that so effectively that it's as if he gave us a detailed assignment without opening his mouth. While he occupied the receptionist, we split up and each went down one wing, making a quick note of the names on the doors. We exited through self-locking doors at each end and met back at the car. Wally joined us.

"What'd you get?" he asked.

"Not much," I said, producing my list. There was nothing close. Wally agreed, but when we looked up from my list, Margo was still studying hers and Lyssa Jack was approaching.

Margo moved to hide her list as Lyssa got close, but Wally said, "It's all right, let her see it."

We leaned on the trunk of Wally's car, studying

138

seven names Margo had scribbled on the back of the envelope containing our home phone bill.

G. Hudak
J. Moran
P. McGlyn
B. Norrin
P. Grace
F. Fayette
T. Perkovich

"All males?" Wally asked.

Margo shook her head, pointing to the last name. "Perkovich is a woman at the end of the hall, over there."

We looked to the end of the east wing. "All the rooms have windows facing the lot here?" Wally asked.

She nodded. "They're odd numbered, beginning with one-oh-one, that's Hudak, through one-thirteen, that's Perkovich."

"You see any of 'em?" Wally asked.

She shook her head. "It was all I could do to get the names. I had the feeling you were being kicked out and the receptionist was sending the gendarmes."

We all smiled. Well, three of us did anyway. Lyssa was still hunched over the envelope with the names on it.

Wally suddenly turned serious and leaned over her shoulder. "Notice something?" he asked, as a chauffeured limousine wheeled into the lot and slid to a stop.

"Maybe," Lyssa said quietly, resolutely, without turning — as Wally did — to see Shirley Walsh emerge from the limo.

The driver stayed in the car as Shirley approached Wally and turned him around by the elbow so she was standing between him and me and had her back to Lyssa.

"Is that Lyssa Jack?" she asked in a whisper.

"Well, yes," Wally said, "but —"

"I figured this was your last resort. He's here, isn't he? Did you find him?"

"No, we didn't, and —"

"*I* did," Lyssa intruded. "What do *you* want with him?"

"I'm in love with him," Shirley said, her eyes steely and her voice quavering.

"Then this ought to be interesting," Lyssa said.

"What's going on?" Wally demanded. "What do you mean you found him?"

Lyssa held up Margo's scribbled envelope and pointed triumphantly to the fourth name. "B. Norrin," she announced, "has to be Byron Norrin Huttmann. And if Margo figured right, he's in one-oh-seven."

Shirley Walsh headed for the entrance, but Lyssa quickly caught up with her. "Use your head," she said. "You'll never get past the receptionist, and it's obvious Byron doesn't want anyone, especially us, to know he's here. I don't know what's wrong with him, but if you want to get to see him, don't go knocking on his door. Let's work together, and we'll both see him."

Shirley was glaring at Lyssa as if she'd just as soon have punched her out.

"Think about it," Lyssa said. "Instead of asking to see him and getting everyone all suspicious, just see if you can get down that hall unnoticed and open the door at the end of the wing. Let me in and give me a minute with him, and I'll see if he wants to see anyone else."

Shirley looked at Wally, as if hoping he'd intervene. He held up both hands and shrugged, smiling sheepishly at Margo and me. "I'm out of this one," he said. "I'll take on two thugs with weapons before I'll take on two women in love with the same man."

140

"I'm not sure I'm in love with him anymore," Lyssa said. "I just want to find out what's going on."

"*That's* your problem," Shirley said, and she strode for the entrance.

"You gonna open the door at the end of the hall?" Lyssa asked. "It's the only way. I'll be waiting."

"Don't hold your breath," Shirley called over her shoulder.

Lyssa hesitated, then scampered toward the door at the end of the wing. Margo started after her, then spun around, as if not sure which woman to follow. Wally motioned to her to just stay put. "Let's just watch," he said. "If Lyssa's found him, we'll know soon enough what it's all about."

"How?" Margo asked.

"If Shirley gets past the receptionist, we can head toward the door where Lyssa's waiting. If she doesn't, we can head back into the lobby to find out what the receptionist tells her."

But even Wally's well-laid plans weren't perfect. Shirley eluded the receptionist, but she had no plans of opening the far door for Lyssa. She headed straight for room one-oh-seven, near the middle of the wing, so while Wally and Margo and Lyssa and I watched through the window, she alone tried the door of the private room.

It was locked, so she knocked loudly. Which brought the receptionist running. Wally gave a final, futile yank on the door at the end of the hall and then ran to the front of the building, through the lobby, and down the hall, the three of us at his heels.

"What *is* going on here?" the receptionist demanded. "Mr. Norrin is to have no visitors. If you had an ounce of human compassion, you'd leave the poor man alone."

141

Shirley looked as if she'd been kicked in the stomach. "What's wrong with him?" she asked, hardly audibly.

The receptionist pursed her lips and lifted a folded card attached to the door. It read, "ACUTE LYM-PHOCYTIC LEUKEMIA."

"What's the prognosis?" Wally asked.

She stared warily at him. "Who's asking?"

"Friends," he said. "We're all friends."

She reluctantly pointed to a set of initials just above the listing of his attending physician. "R.F.," was the notation.

Wally looked into her eyes, asking the question without speaking.

"Rapidly fatal," she said. "I believe he has a few weeks."

"I don't believe it," Lyssa said, almost shouting. "How could it happen so fast?"

"It can," the woman said. "Now be quiet."

The door opened and a pale, thin, exhausted looking young man in a terrycloth robe gazed out at us. "Yes, it can," he said weakly. He appeared a bit puzzled by all the commotion, but it seemed he had us all figured out as he took in the scene.

He had known Lyssa had private investigators look-ing for him, and he couldn't hide his disappointment that she had found him. He ignored her and his face contorted into a pathetic combination of smiling and weeping as his eyes rested on his real love.

"Shirley," he said softly, and she embraced him and led him to a chair. Margo reached in and shut the door behind them, and Lyssa Jack ran from the building, sobbing.

EPILOGUE

Byron was, of course, cleared of any suspicion in the death of Collin Walsh, whose demise was attributed to a heart attack.

Byron and Shirley were finally able to openly declare their love for each other, and Byron consented to a symbolic engagement period. He talked Shirley out of marriage, even though she insisted she was willing to be married to him even if only for a few short weeks.

She spent many painful hours with him, yet Wally and Margo and I agreed that loving and being loved by someone other than his immediate family made Byron's final days easier for him.

He told her how he had tried to leave the Faslund company without worrying anyone except Collin Walsh. He had moved and sold his furniture himself when his strength was fair, and he had put extra miles on the rented truck just to throw off anyone who thought to try to trace him that way.

He knew Mr. Walsh had originally included him in his will and that he would soon, of course, remove him for strictly pragmatic reasons. As the old man was not able to change his will in time, Byron passed along his inheritance to his family in Michigan, at Shirley's urging.

Ironically, Collin Walsh had been secretly having a

place prepared for him at his own estate where he could live out his final days if he wished. Shirley—who had not known what all the refurbishing work had been about—checked into the progress on the preparations, but Byron deteriorated so quickly that he was unable to make the move.

Five weeks and two days after we had found him at LACRI, Byron Huttmann died. Lyssa was bitter for several weeks and told Margo not to waste her breath trying to make it all make sense "from a religious point of view."

But Margo is still on the case, and she plans to use an accomplice. Shirley Walsh. I told Margo I doubted Lyssa would ever want to see Shirley again. But with Margo working on her, who knows?

The Reunion

In a big, double volume, Margo and Philip enjoy a family reunion of sorts, bringing back many of the friends and characters they've encountered in the first twelve stories.

Returning will be Earl Haymeyer, Amos Chakaris, Larry Shipman, Hilary Brice, Allyson Scheel, and many others in a double dose of mystery and intrigue that will keep you reading till dawn!

Moody Press, a ministry of the Moody Bible Institute, is designed for education, evangelization, and edification. If we may assist you in knowing more about Christ and the Christian life, please write us without obligation: Moody Press, c/o MLM, Chicago, Illinois 60610